Emma Leigh Reed

A TIME TO HEAL

Emma Leigh Reed

Copyright © 2015 by Emma Leigh Reed

ISBN-10: 0-9967270-2-7
ISBN-13: 978-0-9967270-2-0

Warning: The unauthorized reproduction or distribution of this copyrighted work is illegal. Criminal copyright infringement, including infringement without monetary gain, is investigated by the FBI and is punishable by up to 5 (five) years in federal prison and a fine of $250,000.

Names, characters and incidents depicted in this book are products of the author's imagination or are used fictitiously. Any resemblance to actual events, locales, organizations, or persons, living or dead, is entirely coincidental and beyond the intent of the author.

No part of this book may be reproduced or transmitted in any form or by any means, electronic or mechanical, including photocopying, recording, or by any information storage and retrieval system, without permission in writing from the author.

Cover Art: Gemini Judson

To Sara

My critique partner, my business partner. Thank
you for always believing in me, for pushing me
when I'm ready to give up and for being my
sounding board. You are truly a blessing in my life.

Chapter One

Kelli Winsor parked her SUV in front of the beat up structure. It wasn't much to look at with the peeling paint, but she knew the interior had recently been renovated. She stepped from the vehicle and crossed the street. The ocean gently lapped the beach and mesmerized her with each crashing wave. Working here was going to be the best move she had made in her life and she knew in her gut that she had finally made a good decision.

She turned back and stared at the building. The sign above the door was worn and couldn't be read. Beau was right when he said the place needed work. When her old friend contacted her to see if she wanted to join him in a business pursuit, she was cynical. Of course she was. She was cynical of everything these days. She didn't trust anyone since her husband left her, not even Beau, to some extent.

Sighing, she mentally made a note of all the work that needed to be done – siding, signage, and window trimming. Once inside, the new tables and newly sanded and polished wooden floors lifted her mood. Kelli was so busy admiring the huge windows that lit the room and the newly renovated bar that she didn't notice Beau standing behind it. A wide smirk spread across his face as she finally caught sight of him. "Glad you finally showed up."

He came around and pulled her into a fierce hug. She'd known him for what seemed like all her life and she hugged back with equal ferocity. "Good to be here."

"Well, what do you think?"

A Time To Heal · 3

"It's a mess outside. You were right about that." Kelli glanced around once more. "But inside looks great."

"I know there's a lot of work to be done. And I know you said you only wanted to be a silent partner, but I really don't mind if you put your ideas out there."

Kelli shrugged. "You don't need me telling you how to run your business."

Beau laughed. His deep voice washed over her with familiarity. "I didn't say tell me how to run the business. I said ideas for renovating."

She smiled and slid onto a bar stool. The idea of moving away from everything had been appealing. The memories-- the hurt and anger-- she'd still brought along, but it helped that she wasn't seeing the familiar haunts she had frequented with her ex-husband.

She shook her head to rid herself of the painful memories and turned towards Beau. "Where do we start?"

4 ·Emma Leigh Reed

He slid a folder across the bar to her. "Here's the inventory I started. Want to start there?"

Kelli shook her head. "That's part of the renovating?"

"No. But we open next week. The outside renovations will be ongoing while we're open for customers."

"Sure, give me the grunt work." She picked up the folder and headed around the bar to start checking bottles.

They worked in comfortable silence. Kelli poked around in the kitchen to familiarize herself with what was available and checked over menu items that Beau had come up with. Simple seafood dishes that suited the bar venue and the casual, beachgoer atmosphere.This had been Beau's dream. He'd always wanted this type of establishment and he was making it happen. He hadn't counted on the renovations being as much as they were, and not wanting to indebt himself, he'd pleaded with Kelli to join him in partnership. She had inherited some money from her grandfather and could afford to invest, even if it didn't start bringing in a profit right off. The location was perfect for her much needed fresh start.

The day flew by as they worked and finally Beau threw some burgers on the grill for them. They ate quietly, lost in their own thoughts. Kelli never had that kind of friendship with anyone else. Beau wasn't afraid to tell her if she screwed up, but he had her back no matter what. She, in turn, was happy to tell him if he messed up—yet he always seemed to have his act together.

Kelli broke the silence suddenly. "Who do you have lined up for a cook?"

"A friend of mine, Dan. He's been through a rough spell, but he's getting his act together."

Kelli shook her head. "Still taking in strays, are you?"

Beau gave her that smile that melted her heart every time. "He lost his wife in a car accident about a year ago. He needs something to occupy his time."

"Okay, but can he cook?"

"Of course." He threw his napkin at her. "Would I bring in someone who couldn't? Have a little faith."

Kelli snorted. "Faith? Yeah, that works well for me."

Beau shook his head. "You've got to let it go. Move on, girl."

Kelli stood and walked to the window. The ocean waves silently crashed onto the sand and she let the image wash over her and take away the stress. "I'm trying. It's not that easy."

"I know it's not." His voice was right behind her and she turned towards him. "In a way, you and Dan have a lot in common. Lost loves can't move on until your allow your heart to heal. You two will be good for each other."

"Don't even think about it. I'm not one of your fixer-upper projects." Her demeanor chilled as her cynical thoughts about relationships bubbled up. This was her time to rebuild her life and forget the past.

A Time To Heal · 7

"I'm not trying to fix you up. But friendship goes a long way when you can understand the other person's grief."

Kelli nodded. She reached up and kissed Beau's cheek. "I'm just thankful you're in my life."

He hugged her close. "You will get through this and you'll see, you'll be stronger in the end."

She caught her breath and just let herself lean on Beau. He had more than enough faith for both of them that she would come out better on the other side. Truth be told, she didn't want to let the anger go. It kept her going, gave her a fire to get up and face each morning, but there were days she physically hurt from the loss of her husband. He may not have died like Dan's wife, but he had walked out and took with him every bit of confidence she had had in herself. She wanted her life back and didn't know where to even begin. Beau was right; this was the new start she needed. It wasn't going to be easy, but she'd push through it and fight to get back the strong, confident, "take on

8 ·Emma Leigh Reed

the world gal" she had lost when she kept quietly
walking on eggshells to keep the peace.

Resolved for another day, she started for the
door. "I will see you tomorrow. I need to settle into
my new place."

Beau smiled. "The key is on top of the door
frame. I stocked your fridge with a few basics."

She punched him in the arm. "Stop trying to
take care of me. I'm here to start standing on my
own two feet, not to mooch off you."

He pretended to fend her off. "It's not a lot and
you're not mooching. Believe me, you will be
earning your keep around here. It's going to be a
while before we pull a paycheck."

She nodded and waved as she headed out the
door. "I know. That doesn't bother me, you know
that."

Beau was letting her stay in the apartment
above the bar while she got settled in her new
environment. She pulled her suitcase from the car
and walked to the stairs on the side of the building.
Her parents would have a heart attack if she had

told them she was co-owner of a bar and going to be living above it. She could hear them now: *No place for a "good girl."* She shook off the voices in her head and climbed the stairs. Beau had warned her it wasn't much and she braced herself for the worst.

Kelli found the key with no problem, unlocked the door and stepped into a living room with a threadbare rug. The couch was worn but plump, giving the appearance of pure comfort. To the right was a small kitchenette. A few steps down the hall was a bedroom with a bed with a bureau and attached tiny bathroom. It was definitely small, but cozy. It was workable. She turned and headed back to the living room. Flopping down on the couch, she sighed and closed her eyes.

Who was this cook Beau had hired and what was his story? Beau had mentioned his wife had died in a car accident. Had his wife been the love of his life and in losing her, was he crippled with grief? Or was his pain caused by the loss of a life that had been replaced, like hers, with going through the motions and just barely surviving a broken marriage? Kelli laughed at herself; she really should have been a writer. She could spin such tales with other people's lives. It was her own soap opera life that was stranger than fiction. It was just too bizarre and unbelievable to think she hadn't seen things for what they were. She flipped to her side and noticed a TV in the corner with an attached note. She stood and reached out to grab it.

No sappy romance movies. Just comedies that will make you smile. Love, Beau

She laughed out loud. Beau knew her habit of falling into the "poor me" and "watch romance all day" mode. She turned from the TV and reached for her phone to put on music that would inspire her to move forward. With music blaring, she started to unpack. Dancing around, moving to the beat, for the first time in a long time.

Chapter Two

Kelli woke to the sound of waves crashing against rocks. She lay with her eyes closed and let the sound wash away her apprehension. Beau had wanted a silent partner, but last night he told her he really needed her to deal with the contractors. She knew he was just trying to keep her busy and was grateful. She'd go crazy otherwise. Pushing back the covers, she rolled out of bed.

She walked to the front of the apartment and stepped out onto the stoop. The sun danced on the ocean. Oh, she definitely could get used to this. The ocean had always been her comfort place, soothing her and bringing her peace. For the first time in almost two years there were no chest pains or anxiety attacks. Maybe she finally *was* moving on. Time to start the day. Turning back inside, Kelli started the coffee maker before jumping in the shower. As the hot water ran down her body, she started a mental checklist. Whether Beau thought so or not, the first order of business was getting the outside cleaned up and a visible, clear sign designed. The bar couldn't function if people didn't know where to find them. She smiled. There was no way she was going to be a silent partner. She had plenty of ideas and was anxious to share them with Beau. And this unknown cook...well, Beau better be right, they needed a good cook. A bar with bad food was not on her radar.

After drying off, she perused her closet and decided on a tank top and a pair of Capris jeans. She pulled her shoulder length hair back in a clip, pondering cutting it, trying a new style.

A Time To Heal · 13

Kelli poured a cup of coffee, closed her eyes and inhaled the rich aroma. She mentally laughed. Her friends in college had made fun of her for smelling her coffee before drinking it. But the scent enriched the flavor for her and she found it comforting. Flipping through the emails on her phone, she enjoyed her coffee until it was time to head downstairs.

As she rounded the corner, she crossed the parking lot to take in the exterior of the building. In the morning light, the paint was more chipped than it had appeared the night before. She narrowed her focus to the sign above. Beau hadn't even told her what he was going to call the place. She frowned. He must have a name ready if he had all the required paperwork filled out and expected to open next week. Minor detail he seemed to have overlooked when talking about this adventure.

The sight of two flat tires on her car stopped her short. They had been fine when she arrived last night. On closer inspection, she found nails in both the front and rear tire on the driver's side. She didn't remember running over them or hearing anything. Obviously they had created a slow leak. She dialed her auto club and arranged to have them come and fix the tires. Just her luck. At least she was here already and it hadn't happened on the road. Not giving the tires another thought, she slipped in the door and again took in the scene. She nodded. The bar, lined with new bar shelves, was stocked and ready to go. The corner stage stood ready for live music.

Voices came from the kitchen. Kelli wondered if Dan, the cook, had arrived. She started towards the door, but stopped when she heard the voices clearly.

"Dan, you've got to be ready for this." Beau's voice was calm, but his irritation laced the words.

"I'm ready. Don't worry, Beau. I'm not going to let you down."

"Good. Kelli will be here shortly and you will be working with her, also."

A Time To Heal · 15

"Silent partner, isn't she? Means I don't answer to her. I'm not having some woman nag and micromanage me."

Kelli shook her head. *Micromanage?* She waited for Beau to correct him, but silence was all that came through. She stepped back when she heard the response.

"I'll deal with Kelli, but you need to know she won't be a completely silent partner, so don't upset her. She needs this."

Kelli clenched her hands by her side. *Needed this?* She was nobody's project and Beau could forget the whole partner thing if he was doing this just to "help" her. Not going to happen. She pushed open the door.

"Am I interrupting?" Kelli worked at keeping the sarcasm out of her voice and couldn't resist lifting an eyebrow at Beau.

She recognized Beau's "Oh shit, I'm in trouble" expression that crossed his face before he smiled. "Never. Come on in. Kel, this is Dan O'Grady. Dan, Kelli Winsor."

16 ·Emma Leigh Reed

"Nice to meet you, Dan." She extended her hand and waited.

Her hand tingled as Dan grasped and shook it firmly.

Ocean blue eyes met hers, eyes she could easily lose herself in. He lingered with his hand in hers for a moment. "Likewise."

She blinked and forced her eyes away and turned towards Beau. "A word, please."

She headed out of the kitchen before he could reply, feeling Dan's eyes on her back as she bounced her ponytail side to side, hoping he liked the view because it may be the last one he got of her. She was fuming when Beau followed her a moment later.

"What's up?" Beau slid onto a bar stool. Kelli stood behind the bar, watching him.

"Want to tell me why I'm really here?"

"You're my partner. You're here to help with the business." Beau stared at her quizzically.

"I'm not a silent partner, Beau."

A Time To Heal · 17

"Okay." Beau tipped his head. "I thought we established that last night."

Kelli curved her mouth up into a bright, tight smile. "That means everyone that answers to you, answers to me."

Beau shook his head. "Crap, Kel. You heard what Dan said?"

"Yup."

"I'm sorry. He's having a tough time. He'll be fine with you once he gets settled in. Don't be too hard on him."

Kelli shook her head. "Too hard on him? Really, Beau? You know me better than that. What is it that you're not telling me about all this?"

"What do you mean?" He stood and moved around the bar. He picked up a rag and wiped down the already clean surface.

"Damn it, Beau. Don't play games with me. I'm not in the mood to be blindsided by problems that could be avoided by you telling me the truth."

Beau threw down the rag as he came around the baar to her side and grabbed her arm. Propelling her

18 ·Emma Leigh Reed

to the other side of the room, he shushed her as they walked.

Kelli stopped short. "Spill it."

"Kel, don't get all huffy. Dan's had a tough time. His wife was killed in a car accident. He's struggling with it, that's all."

"There's more to it than that and you better tell me what's going on."

Beau glanced towards the kitchen. He faced Kelli and kept his voice low. "His wife was killed in a car accident after they had argued. Things were angry between them and he feels guilty."

"Okay." Kelli stared at him. "And? That seems an extreme reaction for him to have to me because his wife died after an argument."

"Kel, it's…well, he was in an accident the same night. He was hit by a drunk driver."

Kelli was baffled. "I still don't understand why he's upset that I'm here."

"It's not you. He just wants to stay away from women right now. He doesn't trust them. You can

A Time To Heal · 19

relate to that since you don't trust men all that much right now either."

"Okay, that I get. But it still seems like there is more to it."

Beau surprised her with a bear hug that nearly crushed her ribs. "Someday I will tell you the whole story, but right now be gentle with him. Can you do that?"

She gave him a squeeze before pulling back. "Fine. Can we get started on contractors and prioritize what needs to be done? Like, the outside work being number one."

"It's all yours. There is a list of contractors behind the bar. Go at it, kid." Beau reached over the bar and pulled out a file filled of phone numbers and names.

"I'll work upstairs. Don't want to scare anyone with my presence." Kelli slapped Beau on the arm with the folder. "Anyway, apparently I ran over a couple of nails and now have two flat tires. My auto club should be here shortly to fix them."

Chapter Three

Kelli spent the next few hours making calls and arranging meetings to get the work started. Drat, she forgot to ask Beau the name of the bar. *There is no reason to not trust Beau. He's never broken your trust. He must have a good reason for leaving out that small detail.* Kelli shook her head. It had to be just an oversight. She finished jotting down notes and put the folder back together. Arms overhead, she stretched. The subtle snapping in her back and neck reminded her she needed to get up and move

A Time To Heal · 21

before getting too stiff, a lingering effect of a car accident she had suffered a few years prior.

The thought of the accident brought her mind to Dan. Was she letting her distrust of men cloud her thinking, or was something off? The past two years she'd given up trusting her own instincts. Her gut feelings had been proven wrong over and over again.

She entered the bar and took in Dan's quick appraisal of her before muttering something to Beau and heading to the kitchen.

"Well, he's just full of sunshine, isn't he?"

"Let it go, Kel." Beau pointed to the folder. "Good progress?"

"Yup. Contractors lined up to scrape and paint the outside. We need signage, though, and should I be bothered that you haven't mentioned the name of this place, yet?"

Beau chuckled. "I didn't tell you during our phone conversations because I wanted to see your face. I'm calling it 'The Salty Claw.'"

Kelli felt her jaw drop. "You're kidding, right?"

"Come on…you always said we should have a place named after that nasty lobster claw you had when we were kids, Mr. Salty." Beau grinned at her.

She shook her head, trying to keep her grin from exploding. "Do you have to remember *everything* I have ever said to you?"

"On a serious note, a good friend of mine has his own sign business. He's designed the sign as a grand opening present to me and it should be delivered this afternoon. See? I can tend to some things without you."

Kelli glanced around. Everything was shiny and new. "Did you advertise for the opening?"

"Yes, doors open at four Friday afternoon and it's been advertised in the local paper for the past couple of weeks. I'm hoping we will have a good turnout. Our normal hours will be eleven to two a.m. Closed on Mondays."

A Time To Heal · 23

Kelli nodded and turned back to Beau. "So are you ready for this? Your big dream turning into reality?"

"Absolutely."

Kelli pointed to the corner stage. "Do you have a band coming for opening night?"

"I have a CD that a guy dropped off. I just haven't listened to it yet." Beau shrugged. "It wasn't high on the priority list."

"But it would bring in more people, I'm sure." Kelli held out her hand. "Let's have it and I'll give it a listen and hope to God it's decent."

Beau slid the CD across the bar. "When is the outside work starting?"

"Tomorrow. I worked my charm and with any luck, it will be freshly painted before opening night. The sign will be here today, you said?"

Beau nodded. "Looks like you have things well under control."

"Building-wise anyway." Kelli nodded towards the kitchen.

"Come on, Kel. He'll come around."

24 ·Emma Leigh Reed

She slid off the barstool. "If you say so." She stared at the kitchen doors, debating whether to go in and try and make conversation with Dan. Shaking her head, she turned towards the exit. "I'll see you in a bit. I'm going to take a walk along the water and clear my head."

Kelli walked the beach, ankle deep in the water, flip-flops in hand. The water was so much warmer in North Carolina than New England. One more reason she could get used to being here. The soft lapping of the waves soothed her nerves. She inhaled deeply the scent of the salt air and let go of the last of the tension that had been plaguing her since she arrived. She thought of the CD Beau had given her to listen to. A local band would bring in more customers, thirsty customers, and really, it all came down to how much people drank while they were at their establishment. She allowed her mind to imagine a drop-dead gorgeous guitar player giving her a chance at another life, a chance to live a different lifestyle. She shook her head. She needed to be practical and logical.

A Time To Heal · 25

She came upon a small area of rocks and climbed up to a dry spot, sat down and closed her eyes. The sounds of the waves crashing against the rocks relaxed her further. The CD of ocean waves she owned wasn't the same as hearing it first hand.. She opened her eyes and a movement to her left showed Dan coming around a rock, unaware she was there.

"Hey." She spoke softly, not wanting to startle him.

"Oh. I didn't know you were here." He stopped.

"I'm sorry if this is a place you come to…I can leave." She started to stand and sank back onto the rock when he gestured for her to stay.

"No biggie. I can come back."

"Don't leave, Dan. There's enough room for both of us." She closed her eyes, not wanting to meet his eyes, those blue eyes that threatened the end of her.

"Looks like you enjoy the ocean as much as I do."

Kelli opened her eyes at his voice next to her and said, "It's pure heaven for me. The best way to relax and de-stress when things aren't going that great."

He nodded, but was silent. Kelli watched him from the corner of her eye, trying not to stare. She swallowed hard and looked at the ocean. Damn, it was the same blue as his eyes.

"Look…I know you heard what I said to Beau. Don't take it personally." Dan turned to face her.

Kelli met his eyes. What a mistake. "What's the deal? You don't know me, why hate me already?"

He sighed and looked out to the water. "I don't hate you. Like you said, I don't even know you. It's just…I don't know. It's easier to hate everyone around me, especially females, at this point."

"She leave you?" Kelli knew the answer, but needed to hear it from him.

"She died, car accident." The bitterness that laced his words startled her.

"I'm sorry."

"Yeah, well, I guess sometimes karma is a bitch." He stood and started down the rocks. "Just don't take it personally, okay?"

Kelli just watched him go. The anger exuding from him surprised her. Maybe her life wasn't as bad as she thought. After all, she just had a cheat of an ex-husband, but her anger had fueled her passion to change her life, while his just seemed to be burning him alive.

Dan entered his house. He glanced around at the sparsely furnished, uncluttered space. A young woman came in once a week to clean. The only area he insisted she didn't touch was the kitchen, where he spent most of his time. Cooking was his stress relief. His kitchen was filled with the best cookware and utensils money could buy. He spared no expense when it came to his passion.

Sprawled out on the couch, Dan replayed his last night with Mia over and over again.

He pushed the food around his plate. Dinner had become a chore to eat together and more nights than not they ate in silence. It killed him to have their relationship this way.

"How was work today?" He set his fork down and watched his wife.

"The usual." Mia continued to eat without looking at him.

"I'm thinking of taking a few days off next week; maybe you could take some time and we could go away for a few days."

Mia's fork clattered on the plate. "Really?" Sarcasm dripped from her lips. "Because my job isn't as important as yours so I can just drop everything at your whim?" She slammed the wine glass down and Merlot splattered. She shoved back her chair and stood.

"I never said that." He reached for her hand, but she sidestepped away.

They stared at each other. Another impasse, just like all the other fights they'd had lately.

"I can't be here right now." Mia grabbed her pursed and started for the door.

Dan followed her. "Where are you going?"

"Out. I love you, but I can't do this. I need a break."

He stood there and listened to the squeal of the tires. They fought a lot lately. He never doubted his love for her, but their marriage had been rocky since day one. Now, five years into it, it felt like it was completely falling apart. There was a finality in her angry words. The anger was underlying even in a seemingly normal conversation.

Dan thought back to their time of dating. At the time, he knew he had done the right thing convincing her to get married when they found out about the pregnancy. She lost the baby only days into the marriage. Resentment from the past five years oozed out of her in every conversation. He couldn't make this work anymore, not if she didn't really want it.

He resigned himself to tell her he was willing to file for divorce if that was what she wanted. The more he thought about it the more he realized there were very few happy times in the past five years together. He had always loved Mia, right from the beginning. He had pushed for the marriage thinking love would come for her, too, once they were married. It struck him she rarely said she loved him and if she did it was a "love you, too" in response to his claims of love. Her saying those words before she left tonight gave him hope that maybe it wasn't over. Maybe she didn't want out, but didn't know how to make it work.

Dan groaned, pressing his palms to his eyes, trying to clear his head of the memories. There was no closure for him. Why couldn't things have ended differently?

Chapter Four

Kelli's day started with her usual routine of enjoying the rich aroma of her coffee before her first sip. After that first sip, she placed the CD of the local band in the player. The guitar filled the room with a familiar rock song. She tapped her foot as she enjoyed her coffee. The music itself was great. The vocals, well, she could get used to them. The lead singer had a gravelly deepness that entranced her. The music was basic with just drums, guitar and a bass. It was simple and good. This band would be great for opening night. Kelli hoped Beau would agree. He had the stage for them. Beau had put the idea of the band on hold for opening night, but Kelli thought it was the perfect touch to ensure a good crowd. She had half a mind to call them and get them lined up, but didn't want to overstep her boundaries of silent partner. A conversation was needed with Beau this morning.

Kelli placed her washed coffee mug in the drain as her cell phone went off, indicating a text message. Aaron, her ex-husband. She received a lot of messages lately, ones she kept ignoring. She missed him, so much at times it was a physical pain, but their relationship had been toxic. With him gone for almost two years now, she could see clearly how bad it had been. She always tried to do the right thing and keep the peace, but looking back, he was selfish, never caring about what she wanted or needed. *Didn't she deserve to have someone in her life that wanted her to be happy, that wanted her to be their priority?*

A Time To Heal · 33

She ignored him once again, slipping the phone into her pocket. She couldn't deal with him now. She rounded the corner, finding scaffold set up. Three men were standing near a van sipping coffee and chatting. It had slipped her mind that they were going to be here today to start scraping the old paint.

A tall man broke from the group of men and made his way towards her. "You must be Kelli. Name's Tom. We spoke on the phone yesterday."

"Hi, Tom. Nice to meet you." Kelli shook his extended hand. "Glad to see you're all set up to start. You let me know if you need anything."

"We'll be starting in just a second. My guess is we'll be ready to start the painting 'morrow."

"Sounds great." Kelli started to turn towards the front door.

"Is that your car over there?" Tom stopped her.

"Yes."

"Looks like there might have been a bit of mischief going on last night."

Kelli jogged over to the car. All four side windows had been smashed. Uneasiness ran over her and she tried to shake it off. Could the flat tires have been intentional? Who would want to vandalize her car? She nodded to the other men before heading inside. Things for the business at least were falling into place.

Beau wasn't in sight when she entered. Turning toward the kitchen, she hoped it wouldn't lead to another confrontation with Dan. He had been almost sociable yesterday on the rocks. She pushed open the kitchen door and found it empty. He had to be here, the door had been unlocked. Coffee was made, she noticed. She poured herself a cup and turned to lean against the counter. She took in the newness of the room. No money had been spared when Beau furnished the necessities. An open bottle caught her eye on the counter across the kitchen, near the clean dishes. Vodka. Who would have an open bottle of vodka in the kitchen?

Dan stepped into the kitchen just as Kelli walked out. He hesitated. She had gotten under his skin and it was getting harder and harder to act like he hated her. A brokenness surrounded her, reminding him of the heartache he felt daily. Yesterday when he went to his place at the rocks, his spot to relax, and saw her there, irritation washed over him. He didn't want to share it, but she had looked so peaceful with her eyes closed—almost happy. Beau hadn't mentioned her story, only that she had been through a rough time. A white mark on her ring finger indicated a ring was recently removed. He glanced around the kitchen and noticed the vodka. Crap. Had she seen it? He needed to be more careful about leaving it around, but he thought he was alone this morning. He'd been going through recipes for different seafood dishes. The menu would be finalized today at his meeting with Beau and he wanted perfection coming from his kitchen.

He shook his head. She haunted his already sleepless nights. He didn't want to see her in his dreams. It was hard enough forgetting Mia, especially with her family calling him all the time. He was tired of playing the part of grieving husband. In reality, he was pissed at Mia. Not only had she walked out on their marriage, but she had almost killed him by driving drunk. Her family had no idea she was the driver of the other vehicle, assuming they were in the same car when the accident occurred. Her family was furious when Dan wouldn't go after the other driver. Dan simply told them the other driver died at the scene. But why was he protecting her? Why couldn't he tell them that Mia had hit him? She *was* the drunk driver that they wanted justice from so badly.

He knew deep down he'd never betray that information. It would kill Mia's mother. As much as Mia had her faults, he wanted her parents to remember the good in her, not what she had become. If only he could remember that good also, not the hateful things she said to him the last few months--the constant bickering and tearing each other down. He sighed. It would be a cold day in hell before he forgot the spiteful person Mia had become during the past few years.

His thoughts returned to Kelli. Although exasperating sometimes, she really was a breath of fresh air to him. Her personality pulled him to her and he found himself becoming more frustrated with the fact that he was finding less and less he could be mad about with her here. Beau had done a good thing bringing her into the business. She was smart and had a good sense of what needed to be done. Under her tutelage, the business would thrive. Closing his eyes, he tried to block her from his mind. She had taken up a permanent residence in his thoughts. The constant battle raged in him of wanting to let go of Mia and allow himself to enjoy life as it was now, fighting with the guilt that held him captive in his past.

Dan turned his focus to the kitchen. He threw himself into his work--a familiar routine that kept him from thinking too much. Pulling his recipe cards towards him, he went over the new items he wanted to add to the menu and did a final check on them. Cooking gave him a contentedness he had never experienced with anything else. He was proud of the work he produced and his love for creating new dishes showed in everything he made. As thoughts of Kelli started to creep into his mind, he turned his attention to a new dessert. Without fail, visions of her eating his cheesecake, her lips sliding it off the fork slowly, just about did him in, and he threw the recipe cards aside. Damn, something had to give soon.

The next few days went by like a whirlwind. Kelli convinced Beau to hire the local band for the opening night. Until Beau was convinced it would be good for the business, he hadn't wanted to invest in a PA system. Luckily, the band had everything they needed. Kelli was hoping they would be a regular until they could line up some additional local talent. The painting outside was finished. The building now looked worthy of the grand opening that was fast approaching.

The lobster claw sign was hung proudly, announcing the new bar in town. Seafood, cold drinks and live music…what more could anyone want? Kelli grinned, thinking of the progress and how impressed Beau was. Silent partner—not a chance. Beau had settled into wanting to be a bartender and gladly stepped aside for Kel to take over the actual managing. She thrived on it.

She and Dan had even come to a silent truce at work. Although he seemed pretty unhappy to see her whenever she stepped into the kitchen, she learned to ignore him. They had not seen each other again at the rocks and Kelli found it to be a great place to unwind. If she was truthful, she secretly hoped Dan would show up, and she tried to ignore the disappointment that sliced through her whenever he was a no-show.

Kelli found a renewed energy and motivation to recapture her old self. She began running again, pushing herself to increase her time. She hoped that by the end of summer she'd be the toned and in-shape self she had been in years past. Coming back from her morning run, she stopped across the street from The Salty Claw. It was looking good. She and

Beau had talked about next summer possibly adding on the front for an outdoor section of seating, moving the live music outside. It was a year away, but loving the optimism that both she and Beau had for this venture spurred Kelli to start making longterm plans for not only the bar, but for her life here in North Carolina.

Chapter Five

Dan headed to his rocky get-away every night and seeing Kelli there, he couldn't bring himself to join her. He would walk away each night and then kick himself when she filled his thoughts. She had him questioning his relationship with Mia. *Had they just been together for the sake of the baby? Had they ever truly loved each other at all?* Their treatment of each other would say they didn't know how to love.

Dan sighed, willing himself to change his thought process. He longed for a drink to take away the pain and dull the memories that bombarded him constantly. He needed to lessen the pain. The alcohol had become his painkiller. As much as he hated alcohol for the role it played in ending Mia's life, he now understood her desire to kill the feelings. He longed for that numbness it brought with the fuzzy memories and lack of desire to remember anything. If only it could stop the images of Kelli from creeping into his thoughts at night and keeping him awake.

Dan turned towards home. The menu was set and he was ready for opening night tomorrow. With a packed place, he would stay busy with food to be sent out. He looked forward to the live music playing. Taking a detour towards his favorite secluded area, he decided he wasn't going to stay away just because Kelli was there. Damn, it had been *his* spot first. He wasn't catering to her just to keep peace.

A Time To Heal · 43

He slowed his steps when he approached,
finding it empty. Frustration hit him with surprise.
He eased down on the rocks and pulled out a bottle
of beer from his backpack. It was almost empty
when he felt her presence.

"Am I interrupting?"

"Nope." Dan swallowed the last bit of beer,
placing the empty bottle in the bag. Drawing out
another one, he held it out to her. "Want one?"

"No, thanks." She sat down a few rocks away,
eyeing him.

"Not going to bite." He took a long swig and
looked at her. "You don't even look remotely
comfortable. Sit over here." He slid over on the flat
surface of the rock. There was more than enough
room for both of them.

She hesitated briefly before joining him.
"Ready for opening night tomorrow?"

"Yup. Should be good." Silence surrounded
them like a thick cloak. "Heard you got a band
coming."

"They sound really good on the CD. Here's hoping they're just as good in person." Kelli turned and faced him. She took a deep breath, trying to form the right words. "Look, Dan, I need to ask you something and I don't want you taking it the wrong way."

Dan straightened his shoulders. "What's that?"

"The vodka bottle open in the kitchen the other day…was it yours?"

Dan smirked, his eyes staring into hers. "Yup. Was trying a new recipe with a vodka sauce. Is that okay with you?"

Kelli let out the breath she had been holding. "Yes. I just, well, I don't want you drinking on the job."

Dan gave a small laugh. "It's a bar. Lots of people are going to be drinking, honey."

"Not while they work and I'm not your honey." Kelli stood, starting off the rocks. She turned, looking back at him. "And the way you are pounding them back right now makes me wonder if you have a problem."

A Time To Heal · 45

Dan stood. "I don't have a problem except for a wanna-be boss who thinks she can micromanage me. Back off."

Kelli's face flushed red, her struggle apparent. Dan kept his eyes on her. He felt like an ass for his behavior, but couldn't seem to control the words that slipped off his tongue. He simply stared at her as she turned away to walk stiffly down the beach.

Dan curled his hand into a fist and opened it slowly. What was it about her that drove him absolutely insane? He understood where she was coming from, but she didn't know he really was bordering on having a drinking problem. He wanted to do nothing more than to go back home, shut himself away and drown his guilt and anger in a bottle. He watched her walk down the beach at a fast clip, fury rolling off her. The familiar feeling of guilt hit him, though this time it was for hurting Kelli. Would he ever be able to have a conversation with her without pissing her off? Probably not. He finished his second beer and zipped up the backpack.

Kelli stretched, feeling the breeze brush across her skin as she kicked off the covers. His lips brushed over her collarbone as he moved further down. She ached with need as his hands caressed her, his fingertips teasing her nipples. She angled towards him, wanting to feel his hard body pressing against her. A soft moan escaped from her lips as his hand glided down her body, coming to rest on her hip. She sat up with fright at the sudden boom of thunder. Glancing around, she realized she was alone. Lying back against her pillow, she sighed. How she missed sex—not so much her ex-husband, but she missed sex. Two years was a long time to be alone.

Listening to the rain pounding on the roof, she glanced at the clock. 12:00…it was going to be a long night. There was no way she'd be sleeping after that dream. The man in her dream had the bluest eyes she had ever seen. She had always been a sucker for blue eyes, but these were ocean-blue, calling her to dive in. She wracked her brain to think who had eyes like that. She only could recall one person—and he didn't even like her. *Dan.* When Beau introduced them, she had all she could do not to stare. They were cold when they looked at her, yet something about them beckoned her. Great, and now she was dreaming of him, and not just a mindless dream. No, the dream was in the most intimate way possible.

She made her way to the living room to sit in the window. Thunderstorms always fascinated her. They invoked memories of her favorite person, her grandfather, who had long since passed. She missed him dearly and wished she could still talk with him. No matter how much she screwed up, he would have always been on her side with no condemnation or judgment. He understood her rebellious nature and even at times encouraged it, telling her to take chances and live.

The grand opening was today and Kelli couldn't afford a sleepless night. She sighed and watched the lightning illuminate the sky. She longed for the comfort of someone who loved her, who would hold her and tell her everything was okay. Those days were gone. Her grandfather had passed when she was in high school and she never had a close relationship with her parents. Beau was her only close friend left after the mess of her marriage. She closed her eyes. She dozed off and on through the rest of the night until the bright morning light woke her.

Kelli moved at a snail's pace – or so it seemed to her. She had been up most of the night with her mind racing. She leaned against the counter, waiting for the coffee maker to finish. The aroma already was invigorating her, clearing the fogginess.

At least her mind was off Aaron, of late. Instead, she was haunted by pain-filled ocean blue eyes. She shook her head. The beep of the coffee maker signaling her life juice was ready brought her back to the present. She poured a mug full and doctored it up. Wrapping her hands around the mug, she inhaled the magic with her eyes closed. A soft sigh escaped her as she took that first sip. Her shoulders relaxed, the warmth spreading through her.

For the first time in a long time, the feeling of belonging somewhere overtook her. She stood on her small deck watching the waves lap the beach as she nursed her coffee. Life could be good here, she just knew it.

Chapter Six

Kelli slipped into the kitchen and watched Dan talking to his kitchen staff regarding the night – opening night. Wow. It had been a whirlwind week, but everything came together quickly, without too many glitches. The newly painted outside gleamed. The advertised band playing tonight was in the bar setting up and doing a sound check. She prayed everything would go smoothly.

Dan stopped talking and stared at her. "Need something?"

"Nope, just wanted to check to make sure you were all set."

"Yup, I'm good." He dismissed her without another glance.

Kelli sighed. Would they ever be able to have a conversation without icicles forming? She swept through the bar and dining area doing a quick check on last minute details. The band was warming up and she felt a sense of peace and excitement with what the evening could hold. This was it—a new beginning for both her and Beau. Beau's dream of owning his own bar was coming true and Kelli only could dream of a brighter future and hopefully another chance of happiness.

At four o'clock they opened the doors for business. A steady line of customers arrived until about six and suddenly the flood gates opened. All tables were full. Kelli and Beau were swamped; Beau tending bar and Kelli seating people and keeping the waitresses on task and customers happy. The music was a hit. Kelli sat down on a stool she had brought over to the door. There was a line forming outside and the house was full to capacity. She grinned. If this was any indication of how things were going to be, they would need to expand before long. The outdoor seating was going to be a must and she made notes to talk to a contractor about how much it would cost to get that done in a rush.

The music swept over her. The rocking rhythm reminded her of her childhood. The guitar brought her back to a happier time when her grandfather played for her. She smiled, thinking that the band members weren't bad to look at, either.

Two a.m. and the doors were finally closed once again. They had been busy since they opened. At this rate, they were going to need another waitress soon, as the staff just couldn't keep up with the unexpected pace this early in the game. Tonight all four waitresses were on. Tomorrow, or later this morning after some sleep, she would post a help wanted sign in the door. Beau agreed it was needed and even mentioned hiring on a second bartender.

A Time To Heal · 53

The instant success of The Salty Claw was overwhelming, but exciting.

"Good night, huh?" Beau glanced around one more time. "Ready to head out?"

"Yeah, on both accounts." Kelli linked her arm through his. "It's going to be a great ride."

"Absolutely." Beau said, pulling the door closed behind them, locking it. Pulling Kelli into a hug, Beau gave her his usual quick kiss on the lips. "Glad you're here. Need me to walk you home?"

"Ha ha. I think I've got it. See you in a few hours."

Kelli climbed the stairs to her apartment and let herself in. It had been a long night and one with little sleep the night before. She slipped into bed, praying sleep would come soon. Laying with her eyes closed, all she could see was Dan's ocean-blue eyes. She sighed and rolled over. Not again. She needed sleep so badly, not a night of haunted dreams of desire and intimacy with a man that hated her. And yet, she felt more and more drawn to his dark, mysterious side.

Excitement ran through Kelli after the success of the opening night. It was going to be crazy with tonight being Saturday. People complimented the bar last night, promising to tell all their friends, and she anticipated another busy night. They opened doors at eleven this morning with a steady flow through the lunch break.

Kelli talked to the waitresses and all seemed to be happy with the flow of the night before. She pulled her blond hair back into a clip and brushed on some mascara before giving herself one more glance in the mirror. The mascara made her green eyes look even greener. She had run upstairs to change after the lunch rush when a new waitress had spilled a drink down the front of her. The girl had been horrified. Of course, it never would have happened had she been watching what she was doing instead of gawking at the cute young guys who had just come in.

No harm, really. One of the perks of living upstairs from the bar. Quick change and touch up of her makeup and Kelli was good to go again. Walking into the bar, she glanced around and found most of the tables full. Kelli walked over to the bar, standing at the end.

"Where's Olivia?"

Beau shook his head. "She quit shortly after you went to change. Decided she wasn't cut out for waitressing. Apparently, it cuts into her flirting time."

"Great. We're swamped and have no other waitresses on staff to call in." She reached behind the bar, grabbing an extra apron. "Looks like I'm waiting tables tonight."

"You sure?"

"It's like riding a bike. I got it." Kelli tied the apron.

Within a couple of hours, Kelli had a renewed respect for the waitstaff. It had been years since she waitressed, forgetting how demanding it was, physically and mentally. The bar was mobbed and people were demanding.

She entered the kitchen. "Where's my food for table five?"

Dan scowled at her. "Another couple of minutes. Can't you just wait your turn like everyone else?"

"You can't be falling behind. If you can't handle it, maybe you need help."

Dan slid finished plates up on the shelf under the warmer. "Here. Get off my back. Tend to your tables and let me deal with the food."

Kelli double checked her ticket as she put the plates on a tray. "Yeah, okay. Just get it done."

She turned to leave and heard Dan mumbling under his breath about her. Kelli shook her head and moved into the dining room. That man was so infuriating. What was his problem, anyway?

Kelli moved from table to table taking orders and bringing drinks. She avoided the kitchen as much as possible. Dan was backed up with orders, and although they were steadily leaving the kitchen, it was obvious that he needed help.

"Deb, you can get your bisque while I work on these other orders." Dan barked out to the other waitress.

Kelli slipped around the other side of the work station. "How many do you need, Deb?"

"Three."

Kelli scooped out the bowls of lobster bisque and handed them over the counter to the waitress. "Don't mind him."

"Damn, Kelli. Go to the other side. You're in the way."

"I'm in the way? I'm helping you, damn it." Kelli firmly stayed put, ladling out two more bowls. She slid them up on the shelf before moving around to put them on her tray. "Heaven forbid you say thanks."

She exited once again with the sound of cursing coming from Dan. She pushed the limit over the next few hours, helping when she could in the kitchen without getting in his way too much. By the

58 ·Emma Leigh Reed

time one a.m. rolled around, she was exhausted and starved. The bar had slowed down to just a few stragglers.

"Deb, go ahead and go home. You must be exhausted." Kelli wiped off the empty tables.

"You sure?"

"Definitely. Thanks so much for your hard work tonight. I know we're short staffed. We'll get that corrected as soon as possible."

Deb waved. "Thanks for helping me. It's nice when owners don't mind jumping in and pitching in when needed. See you tomorrow."

Kelli sank into a chair. Her legs were killing her. She was too tired to even think about eating now, even though her stomach rumbled in protest. She sighed and stood. Time to finish cleaning up.

Grabbing another full tray of dirty dishes, she took them to the dishwasher. "Looks like that's it out there. Just a few people left, but Beau is cutting them off."

"Did you ever eat?" Dan asked as he started putting away clean pans.

A Time To Heal · 59

"No. And at this point, I don't have the energy."

Dan nodded and turned towards the grill. "Go sit and I'll bring something out to you."

"No need."

"God, really? Think of it as the thanks you were complaining I didn't give you earlier." He dismissed her, putting together some concoction.

Kelli shrugged and headed back to the bar. She slid onto a bar stool, sighing. "Everyone's paid and gone. I locked the door while you were in the kitchen." Beau slid a glass of wine to her. "I'll be in the office, but sit and relax a few minutes. We'll talk when I'm done with the receipts."

Kelli sipped the wine and simply nodded. Her mind wandered to the evening. Leave it to Olivia to walk out on a busy night. She took another drink and set down the wine glass just as a plate was placed in front of her. Dan walked behind the bar and grabbed a bottle of beer.

"Thanks." Kelli looked down at the plate. Shrimp scampi over a bed of rice. She inhaled the scent of garlic. On the side was a helping of marinated mushrooms, cherry tomatoes and mozzarella cheese balls. She stabbed one of the shrimp with her fork and placed it in her mouth. The sweetness of the shrimp combined with the garlic – *heaven*. She closed her eyes and sighed. "Mmm."

She dug into the mushrooms. Tension rolled off her shoulders with each bite of the comfort food. Wow, Dan had outdone himself. She hadn't tried his food before, but *wow* was the only word that came to mind. She met his eyes as he stood across from her watching with a half smile on his face.

"This is delicious." Kelli gushed between bites.

"Glad you like it. There is one slice of cheesecake left. Want it?"

"I shouldn't, but if it's half as good as this…."

Dan placed his bottle down. "I'll get it. You deserve it tonight. You worked hard."

Kelli finished the food and sipped her wine while Dan was in the kitchen, amazed by his compliment. He was full of surprises. And he could

A Time To Heal · 61

definitely cook. Hearing the swish of the kitchen door, she glanced over her shoulder. Dan carried a plate with a slice of cheesecake with fresh strawberries on the top with a drizzle of chocolate sauce. The plate held two forks.

"Two forks?"

"Well, you don't deserve it that much so I thought we'd share it." He waited for her reaction.

Kelli flashed him a smile. "And you think you are deserving of half of this? You were a mess back there tonight."

"A mess? You were in my way." Dan picked up one of the forks and stabbed a good chunk of it. Holding it up, he waved it in front of her. "You think you are more deserving?"

Kelli watched him and moved her head forward slightly to capture the piece of cheesecake in her mouth, slowly sliding the bite off the fork. She licked her lips slowly, savoring the creaminess of the desert.

Her eyes never left his and he swallowed hard. "Hmmmm...heaven." Her words were barely a whisper.

"Glad you like it." He placed the fork down.

"Aren't you going to have some?" Kelli grabbed the fork and took another bite. She closed her eyes, appreciating the flavors of the strawberries and cheesecake dancing on her tongue.

Dan cleared his throat. "I've got to finish cleaning the kitchen. Enjoy."

Kelli watched his back go through the door. It was a like a switch flipped one more time. He could be ornery and then charming and sweet, a real turn on, before he retreated once again.

Chapter Seven

Opening weekend had been a success. Kelli sipped her coffee, thinking over the night. It had been uneventful, a packed house with everyone enjoying the live music. Exhausted from waiting tables, she finally drifted off to sleep about three a.m. and now at seven, she was wide awake and ready to take on the world. Although too tired for a run, she took her coffee cup and made her away across the street to the beach.

It was warm already this morning. Kelli wasn't used to it being in the seventies at seven o'clock. New England definitely was a lot colder and although it got warm during the day, it was never this warm in the morning. She could get used to the North Carolina weather. She loved the warmth heating her skin this early. No one was on the beach. It was only she and the waves communing with each other. Getting out of New England and starting her life over again was a dream come true, one she had almost given up. She smiled. And then came Beau, calling her out of the blue.

Her friendship with Beau never wavered over the years. He understood when she cut ties because her husband didn't want them to talk, although she couldn't deny the ache of missing him. Her ex had pretty much cut off all her friends. She made a mental note to call her friend Jillian to check on her.

Jillian's friendship she had concealed from Aaron. He never knew how close they had become or that she had been giving Jillian money to squirrel away. Jillian had needed to escape. Kelli pleaded

A Time To Heal · 65

with her to come with her to North Carolina, but Jillian's fear of leaving her boyfriend was too great. Their eight year old son, Aiden, begged to go with Kelli, yet Jillian just sat crying while she sported another black eye. Kelli promised to send money when she could, guilt overtaking her for leaving. Aiden broke her heart with his cries as she walked out the door before Sam had arrived home. It would be hell to pay for Jillian if he found Kelli there. He didn't like Kelli encouraging her to get away and Kelli knew if he found out, Jillian could be in real danger.

Kelli checked her phone and realized that she had been sitting on the beach for over an hour. She forced herself to get up and head for home. A quick shower then she was going to get to the bar to check inventory after last night's madness and see what she could do about hiring another waitress.

Pouring another cup of coffee after her shower, she arrived downstairs just as Beau was opening up. "You're here early."

Beau waited for her to arrive at the door. "Wanted to check inventory after last night."

"Looks like we had the same idea. Probably should check with Dan and see how the kitchen went last night, unless you already talked with him."

Beau shook his head no. "He cleaned up and then cleared out pretty quick. He just said everything went fairly smoothly considering."

"Considering what?" Kelli slid into a bar stool as Beau went around.

"Not sure, I'm assuming considering we were busier than we anticipated. I honestly had no idea what to expect, but I didn't imagine a full house the first weekend."

"It was awesome. You should be proud. You obviously did some spot on marketing."

They both turned as the door opened and in walked a young boy and a woman.

"Can I help you?" Beau called from the bar.

A Time To Heal · 67

"Aunt Kelli!" The boy raced across the room, flinging himself into Kelli's arms as she knelt down to greet him.

"Aunt Kelli?" Beau glanced down at Kelli, who hugged the boy tight.

"Beau, this is Aiden and my friend, Jillian." She let go of Aiden to cross the room and pull Jillian into a hug. "How did you get here?"

"I drove all night. It's been exhausting. I got your letter telling me about this place. Long story, but I need a place to stay and a job." Jillian nervously glanced around.

"All I have is one bedroom, but you and Aiden are welcome to stay with me. I'll sleep on the couch until you can find something. Just so happens we are looking for a waitress, right Beau?" Kelli linked arms with her friend and pulled her to the bar.

"We are." Beau held out his hand. "I'm Beau, the co-owner with Kel on this establishment."

Jillian shook his hand. "Nice to meet you. Sorry to barge in before you were open, but once

Aiden knew we were going to see Kelli, well…he just couldn't wait."

"Don't apologize. You know you're always welcome." Kelli pulled her into another hug. "I'm glad you're out."

"Are you guys hungry?"

Jillian shook her head. "We stopped on the way about an hour ago and ate." She ran a hand over Aiden's head, ruffling his curls. "Sorry to show up like this, but it was a last minute decision to leave."

Beau picked up his file from behind the counter. "Jillian, when you and Kel are done catching up, meet me in the office and we'll get you set up for payroll. Can you start tonight or would you rather start tomorrow?"

"Tonight is great. I can do that now. Kel, would you mind getting Aiden settled and I'll be there in a few minutes."

"Of course. Right up the stairs on the side of the building. Come on, Aiden" She held out her hand to the boy who was more than eager to ditch his mom.

A Time To Heal · 69

Kelli snuggled up with Aiden on the couch, holding him close. "Are you okay, bud?"

"Yeah." Aiden curled up closer. "Daddy hurt mom again. I hate it when she cries."

Kelli's chest filled with an ache. She wanted to protect Aiden more than anything. There were just some things in life that a child shouldn't see. She sighed as she closed her eyes and prayed that Aiden and Jillian were finally safe.

Kelli opened her eyes when the door opened and Jillian walked in. "All set?"

Jillian flopped onto the couch beside Aiden. "Yup. Thanks again, Kel. I don't know what I would have done if you weren't here."

"Want to tell me what's going on now?"

"Aiden, why don't you go crawl up onto Kelli's bed and try to sleep for a while?"

Aiden grumbled, but did as he was told. Kelli smiled. "He's getting so big."

"Yeah, he is." Jillian curled up and pulled a throw pillow into her lap. "Sam got out of hand last night." She paused, closing her eyes. "He went after

Aiden. As soon as he went to the store for more beer, we were in the car and gone."

"Wow."

"I'm hoping he slept it off last night instead of trying to find us. That will at least give us more of a head start."

"Jill, does he know where I am?"

Jillian shook her head. "I destroyed your letter after I read it. He doesn't even know we have been in touch."

"Good. Then he has nothing to go on to search for you." Kelli knew his hands were lethal weapons and had seen the evidence too many times of how Jillian had barely escaped them.

Chapter Eight

"Penny for your thoughts?" Kelli smirked as Beau came out of his daydreaming.

"Not even worth a penny."

"Ha, that I believe." Kelli sank into the chair. "I know you hired Jillian based on my friendship with her. Thanks."

Beau waved away the gratitude. "Stop. We have always looked out for each other. Although I will have to say I don't think I did such a great job of looking after you with all you went through with your marriage."

Kelli shrugged. "It is what it is. Move on…isn't that what you're always telling me?"

Beau nodded absently. "What's her deal?"

"Jillian?"

"Yeah."

"I won't tell you the details, but she was in a violent relationship that used to be directed at just her. Apparently last night Sam went after Aiden." Kelli sat silently for a moment. "The straw that broke it all, you know?"

"I get it. I won't ask questions, but do you think he will show up here?"

"I don't think he knows where she is. He didn't know where I went. But I know you're worried about him showing up here. Truthfully, so am I."

Beau stood. "Well, we'll wait and see. Let's check inventory before it's time to open. Time got away from me and now it's almost eleven."

The next hour was hectic. Beau and Kelli worked silently, taking stock of what was used last

A Time To Heal · 73

night and planning another order. Dan handed his list of inventory from the kitchen to Beau.

"When the shrimp came in this morning, I bought extra. That seemed to be the big hit last night."

Beau checked the list. "Sounds good."

Dan glanced at Kelli and without a word turned back towards the kitchen.

"Well, the thaw hasn't begun there yet now, has it?" Kelli stared after him.

"Give him time."

"Yeah, that's what you keep saying. Maybe he just needs a kick in the butt to snap out of it." She shook her head and handed Beau the list she had been working on. "We're open, so I'm going to head over to the door."

"Kel…"

Kelli waved her hand in the air dismissively as she walked off. Thankfully, they were interrupted by a group entering The Salty Claw. Kelli immediately turned on the charm and sat them.

Interacting with the customers brought her joy and she allowed confidence to flow from her.

Kelli spied Jillian coming out of the kitchen as she talked with Beau at the bar. "She must have met Dan." She laughed. "Look at that shocked look on her face."

"What's the deal with Mr. Quiet in the kitchen?" Jillian slid onto a stool next to Kelli.

"Ha. You call him Mr. Quiet, I call him Mr. Miserable. You'll get used to him."

Beau laughed out loud. "Mr. Miserable? That's the best you could come up with? I expected more from you, Kel."

She stuck her tongue out at him. "Oh, there's worse I call him that I just don't share with anyone."

Jillian looked between Beau and Kelli. "He's cute, Kel."

"Don't even go there. I'm not interested."

"Really? Not even in those blue eyes? I know what a sucker you are for blue eyes."

A Time To Heal · 75

"Get to work, will ya?" Kelli stood and headed to the hostess station. She couldn't allow herself the luxury of enjoying those eyes. The pain in them tore straight through to her heart, even if they were the most incredible color blue she had ever seen.

Chapter Nine

Kelli turned to find Aaron standing in the doorway. She stiffened her back and walked towards him. "What are you doing here?"

"I wanted to talk to you. Do you have a minute?" Aaron glanced around before he made eye contact.

Kelli gestured towards a table near the back. "Have a seat. I'll be right over." Kelli moved behind the bar and puttered, wanting to make Aaron wait. She knew she had to face him and headed for his table.

She wasted no time as she slid into the chair. "What's going on?"

"Kel, I screwed up big time. I know that. I miss you and I'm sorry for ever hurting you."

"Okay." Kelli shrugged her shoulders. "Really doesn't matter at this point."

Aaron stared at her. "It does. I want you back. What can I do to fix this?"

"You're kidding. Fix this? I gave you exactly what you wanted–a divorce. Remember? You were so in love with the whore you had been sleeping with you couldn't wait to marry her. I didn't fight you. You got *exactly* what you wanted."

"I was wrong. Kel, I need you in my life."

Kelli had a flash of what life had been like with Aaron. Even when she thought they were so in love with each other, she was never first in his life. They did whatever he wanted, when he wanted. She had walked on eggshells the whole time they were married and she didn't want to do that again. She shook her head. "I was never your priority, Aaron. When I love someone, I give them everything–all of myself, they are first in my life. I deserve someone that loves me as fully as I love them. I need, and want, to be someone's top priority." She took a deep breath. "There will always be a part of me that loves you, but no, you can't come back."

"Kel, at least think about it. Let's talk and spend some time together. I know what we had is still there and we can find it again. You know you can't live without me – never could." Aaron smirked at Kelli. He sat back his eyes never leaving Kelli's.

She stood and touched his shoulder. "Take care, Aaron." The walk to the kitchen stretched out before her seemingly twice as far as it had been only moments before. She bit her bottom lip to stop the threatening tears. She prayed he would be gone before she came back.

"What do you....?" Dan started.

She held up her hand and walked past him to the back door. She slipped through the door just as the tears escaped and coursed down her cheeks. To take Aaron back would have been the easy thing; she would be back in her comfort zone, yet she also knew it was unhealthy. She needed to start over, needed to be happy with herself and her choices. She was strong. She could do this. Kelli wiped the tears away and breathed in deeply. She allowed herself to exhale slowly, letting go of the idea of what love should have been for her. She inhaled again, allowing herself the thoughts of growing stronger and never being the person someone else thought she should be. It was time to be her true self and remember who she used to be.

She squared her shoulders as she returned to the kitchen.

"You okay?" The softness of Dan's question startled her. She met his eyes. Warmth spread through her as she lost herself in those ocean blue eyes, the ones that had been haunting her dreams since she met him.

"Yeah, I'm fine." She shrugged. "Didn't mean to interrupt your space back here."

Dan gave a small smile. "No problem, just don't let it happen again." As quick as anything, the conversation was over as he turned his back, indicating he was done talking.

Kelli stared at him for a moment. Well, that was a breakthrough. Apparently he wasn't all bulldog. She turned on her heel and headed back to the dining room without a word.

Kelli's eyes immediately sought out the table Aaron had been at when she left. Damn, he was still there. Kelli fumed as she turned and walked away from Aaron. She didn't want a conversation with him. She wanted to be on her own—without him in her life in any way, shape or form. He was so full of himself, thinking he was the reason she was anything at all. He had made her believe she could never function on her own and that he was the best thing that had ever happened to her. She kept an eye on him as he sat back and ordered a beer. No, he wasn't leaving quite yet. She contemplated the various reasons he was here, all scenarios ending badly in her mind. Kelli had put up with his attitude.

He had actually thought that he had it made with her taking care of everything while he went on his business trips, and apparently having a totally different life while he was away.

Two beers into the evening, Aaron seemed to be enjoying the music. Kelli was pleasant to the customers and thriving in her role of "hostess." Tension filled her shoulders as she felt Aaron's eyes on her every move. The man infuriated her and the more he kept his eyes trained on her, the more she tensed up. He had been the most selfish man she had ever met during their marriage. Shock had filled her when he had told her that she would never come first before his job. She turned towards the bar and found Beau watching her.

"Trouble?"

"No, not really." Kelli nodded in Aaron's direction. "He thinks he wants me back."

"And?"

Kelli tilted her head at him. "Really? You think I would take him back?"

"I think if you're struggling to please everyone else, you'd consider it."

"Come on, my life's just starting over here."

Beau removed empty beer bottles from the bar and wiped it down. "I think you put on a good front."

Kelli knew he was right. She struggled with the thought that she had tried everything she could and if Aaron hadn't been so adamant about wanting a divorce, she would still be married to him, trying to make it work. In the long run, she knew she made the right decision, but it went against her upbringing to walk away from a marriage.

"I see those wheels turning. You know I'm right." Beau slapped her playfully with the hand towel he held.

"I know. But I'm trying to move forward. It's just hard to know who I am anymore."

"You'll get there. Give yourself time, and don't let him charm you into taking him back. He's not worth it, and you can't tell me the sex was that good."

A Time To Heal · 83

Kelli laughed. "Oh, but it was good." She winked at Beau.

"Give it time. There could be better out there that you just haven't experienced yet." Beau gestured towards the door. "Now get to work or I'll have to can you."

Dan kept his back to her until he heard the door swing shut behind her. He let out a sigh. She was getting under his skin. Pain cloaked her, giving him the impression that she had been hurt bad. For a brief moment, he had a flash that maybe not all women were the jerks that Mia had been at the end. Just as quickly, the guilt hit him. She was dead. How could he think such ill thoughts of her? Regardless of how their marriage had been, he had loved her, and although he was willing to give her a divorce, he didn't want the marriage to end – and certainly not end on the tragic note the way it did. He picked up his glass and downed it. He was careful to hide his drinking at work and keep it to a minimum, but of late Kelli's presence caused an upheaval in what little sense of control he had in his life.

Chapter Ten

Sex had been good between Aaron and her, which is why they had stayed married as long as they had, but Aaron had gotten bored and decided to spice up his life elsewhere. She hadn't known for years until he had gotten stupid and thought he wanted out because he thought he had fallen in love again. He should have known to keep his mouth shut and just continue on like it had been. She had wanted the marriage to work so much that she probably would have put up with anything. Yet she was different now. Her confidence was returning.

Kelli was careful to keep her eyes away from Aaron while she seated people. Thank God it was a busy night. The music was well received and she had lined up the band to play every Friday, Saturday and Sunday nights for the next month. She'd be searching out some other bands for other nights. The band seemed to have a small following that had come and stayed, spending quite a bit on a bar tab. Kelli snuck into the kitchen every half hour or so to try and escape Aaron's eyes as they followed her every move. Dan never said a word, for which she was thankful.

They finally closed the doors. Kelli pushed the broom around the bar area. The waitresses finished cleaning tables and putting chairs up for the night. She wasn't sure what time Aaron had finally left, but heard the waitresses giggling about how charming he was and how he had promised to be back tomorrow night. She groaned. She didn't want

A Time To Heal · 87

him showing up here every night. She made it clear she didn't want him back.

"I think you have that one spot pretty clean." Beau's voice broke through her thoughts.

"What?"

"The rest of the floor still needs sweeping, but that one area you've got spotless." He smirked as he went back to counting up the receipts for the night.

Kelli made short work of sweeping and put the broom away. "How'd we do?" She slid onto a bar stool.

"Good. It was better than I expected. I think the band was a hit."

"They agreed to play every weekend, Friday through Sunday, for the next month. Figured we would go month to month. I'm going to look for some other local talent for week nights."

"Sounds like a plan." Beau put away the receipts and leaned on the counter. "Want to tell me why Aaron hung out here all night?"

"I don't know. I made it clear we were through. The divorce has been final for over a year." Kelli shook her head. "I don't know what his deal is, but he certainly made an impression on the waitresses. They talked about him coming back tomorrow."

"Want me to take him out back and talk some sense into him?"

Kelli stared at him. "I know you're joking, but please don't even say it." She stood. "If you are done with me, I'm headed upstairs and crashing. Jillian already left?"

"Yeah. She was exhausted. I let her go at midnight to get some sleep. See you tomorrow. Need me to walk you to the stairs?"

"No, I'm sure he's gone. Besides, I can handle myself. Those kickboxing classes did some good, you know, beyond weight loss."

Kelli glanced around the parking lot as she walked to the corner of the building. It was empty and she let out a breath of relief. She hoped Aaron wouldn't cause problems. She tiptoed into the bathroom to change, not wanting to wake Jillian and Aiden. She had slipped into a tank top and yoga pants. Settling onto the couch, a knock on the door

A Time To Heal · 89

surprised her. She hesitated for a brief moment. He couldn't have found out where she was living.

Kelli swung open the door and gestured for Dan to come in. "What's up?" She instantly was aware of the thin tank top she wore without a bra.

"I wanted to check on you. You seemed upset tonight, and given the night we had down there, I expected you to be flying high." Dan shut the door behind him.

"It was nothing." Kelli shrugged as she sat on the couch, pulling a throw pillow close to her chest, her arms wrapped around it.

Dan sat down on the couch facing her. "Nothing? Come on, you kept popping into my kitchen like you were hiding from something or someone?"

"Look, sorry if I was interrupting you…"

"Kelli, it's not that. I was concerned."

She watched him. He seemed sincere and damn, those eyes were pulling her in. "My ex showed up."

Dan nodded. "And?"

"And what?" She picked at the corner of the pillow. "I know you think all women are dirt bags, and your wife must have done a number on you, but don't come in here and start acting like I was being a bitch to my ex. You have no idea what the deal is between him and I."

Surprised flashed acrosed Dan's face. "You're right. I don't know your deal, no more than you know mine. I wasn't fishing for your flaws, I just thought...hell, I don't know what I thought." Dan stood and turned to the door.

Kelli walked behind him and didn't have a chance to step back when he turned to face her. Without warning, he put his arms around her waist. She stilled and made the mistake of looking up to meet his eyes. His face was close to hers. Her lips parted as she waited.

"What are we doing?"

"Doing?" Her voice was a whisper and she ran her tongue over her lips, wondering if he was going to kiss her.

His voice was quiet as he moved closer, his lips just above hers. "Do you know what you do to me?"

Before she could answer, he captured her mouth with his. His hand moved up behind her neck, his fingers entwining in her hair. He tipped her head to allow him greater access, his tongue teasing hers. She leaned closer. She knew she needed to break this off and yet logic was not winning over the warmth spreading through her and the need to feel him against her.

He pulled back and she searched his eyes. She was willing, but conflict flashed across his face. "Kelli." He placed his forehead against hers and closed his eyes.

She was quiet. She sensed the turmoil in him and waited for him to work through his emotions. She wanted to pull him closer and hug him until whatever battles he was fighting were won. "I should go. I probably should apologize here, but I'm not going to." He slipped out the door before she said a word.

She closed the door behind him, leaning against it. What was that? He couldn't stand her and yet twice tonight he had shown a compassionate side that threw her. She needed his hard, angry persona, the one that allowed her to stay in that place herself. What a pair they were, obviously full of pain and sorrow—but full of desire, too?

Kelli woke with the sun. Sleep eluded her after Dan left. She couldn't wrap her head around why he even showed up to check on her. She dressed quickly and after tying her running shoes, she stretched.

Although she had had no more than a couple of hours of sleep-- a fitful sleep at that-- she decided the only place to empty her mind from the unending thoughts racing through her head was the beach. She left Jillian a note and headed out. Crossing the street, she started the journey down the sand, running close to the water.

As with other days, her mind's clutter started to clear out with each pounding step. The sound of the waves gently lapping the sand soothed her and the

A Time To Heal · 93

further she ran, the clearer her mind became. Her thoughts drifted to the new bar and the life she was starting here. Kelli switched gears and thought about Aaron and his odd behavior last night, hanging around until closing. No matter how far or how fast she ran, pushing herself to outrun the thoughts, her mind continued to circle back to Dan and his late night visit.

She stopped to rest when she reached the rocks that had become her spot, breathing deeply, pulling the sea air into her lungs. She closed her eyes and listened to the waves.

"I didn't know you were a runner."

Kelli started at the voice. "Just started really when I moved here. You?"

Dan sat on the rock next to her. "I've done a bit. Have you found the trail down the beach, out on the peninsula?"

"No, I usually run in the other direction and back, ending here."

"Someday you should head down that way. You'll know it when you get to it. It was always a favorite place for me to run." Dan twisted the cap of his water bottle on and off. "Look, I don't know what to say about last night. I hadn't planned on that happening."

"Don't worry about it." Kelli stood. "I'll let you have some peace."

"Kelli." He reached for her hand. "I'm sorry for the way I've been. It's not you."

"Yeah, I get that. It's no biggie. We both have issues." She gave his hand a quick squeeze before heading for her apartment. So much for clearing her head. The man was a contradiction.

Chapter Eleven

He hadn't slept last night at all. It had been a stupid move, kissing her like that. But, God, if it didn't feel good to have her against him, tasting her. He shifted his position and swore under his breath. His marriage had been over before the car accident, but he wanted closure. He couldn't possibly think of Kelli in the way he was without letting go of his marriage. It had been years since he felt such an intense desire for someone, and yet she had her own issues, like she said. He didn't need to get involved in that, especially if her ex was back. Maybe her ex had decided to forgive her and take her back for whatever it was she had done. After all, who would let her go in good conscious?

He craved a drink. The pain had increased since Kelli arrived. He needed to dull the ache that consumed him. He wanted nothing more than to have a clear mind and forget about Mia. Although the pain was intensified around Kelli, she also brought to him thoughts of stopping the destructive behavior. He wanted to be a better person; he liked the thought of a better him. It scared the hell out of him to even think of possibly trying another relationship. He couldn't bear it if another woman betrayed him like Mia had. He had no proof that she was having an affair, but he knew that she only married him because of the baby. Probably the worst thing they could have done, but he had really wanted it to work. He truly believed it could work.

What a fool he had been. He knew now that one could not make a marriage work unless the other person wanted it just as much. It was impossible to convince someone to fight for love when they didn't have the desire for it. Why couldn't he have been in love with someone who had loved him just as much? Stretching out his legs in front of him, he lay back against the rocks, soaking in the sun. His mind drifted to the what if's of his marriage. What if Mia hadn't walked out that night? Would they still be together now? Would they have split up eventually? He had been ready to let her walk away, and yet guilt laid like a rock in his stomach, holding him in the past. He sighed and stood. Work was the only passion he had in his life at this moment and it was going to propel him into the future – at what cost, he wasn't yet sure.

The past few weeks had flown by. The bar had been a hit with the locals and was packed every night. Kelli looked forward to Mondays when the bar was closed to have a little free time. She explored the town and found some unique small stores. She had also found the running trail that Dan talked about.

It had become her favorite place to run. The peninsula with the sight of the water on both sides crashing on the rocks gave her a peaceful feeling. The salty spray against her face was a welcome wake up call every morning. The quiet was heaven. It was nothing more than a trail that ran out away from the mainland about two miles. She had upped her running to five miles a day and she was feeling great about herself and her new lifestyle.

Aaron disappeared after the first week of hanging out at the bar. He had approached her numerous times about getting back together and each time she had turned him down. He just didn't seem as charming as he once had been. She dreamt of the ocean-blue eyes of Dan and the way he had kissed her. They had avoided each other since then and she missed seeing him at the rocks.

Her feet pounded the trail of the peninsula and with each step her mind cleared further. Kelli found herself enjoying the sounds of the birds, the gentle water along the trail and the smell of the freshly bloomed flowers. She could get used to this life.

Beau was happy with the way the bar was going and seemed oblivious to the strain between Dan and Kelli and the chemistry that sizzled every time they were around each other. Kelli had stayed out of the kitchen in an effort to avoid seeing those eyes. Damn, those eyes. One look from him and she was flustered, wanting to taste him again.

As she arrived back at the bar, she noticed the kitchen door open. She started that way until Dan stepped outside. He held a glass in his hand and she wondered what he was drinking and hoped it wasn't more alcohol. She couldn't prove he was drinking while at work, and his cooking was a huge hit. He never seemed intoxicated, but she knew that functioning alcoholics rarely seemed inebriated and could manage quite well. Questions filled her mind as to what his wife had done to cause him so much pain.

She turned and headed to her apartment for a shower before work. Beau had things under control and she was enjoying playing the hostess without any real other duties. She helped with the

100 ·Emma Leigh Reed

bookkeeping, but other than that, Beau was well organized and liked to be hands on in the business aspect as well as tending bar. He said it gave him a sense of purpose to be involved with the patrons on a nightly basis. He agreed to hire a second cook to help Dan in the kitchen. Kelli pushed for it, not giving away her misgivings about Dan's drinking if he was able to work. She always did prepare for the worst and wondered more than once if that just made her cynical.

Jillian and Aiden had moved into their own place a few days ago and it seemed strange having the apartment quiet again. Kelli missed having Aiden underfoot, but understood their need for privacy. A one bedroom apartment for three of them was not the ideal situation.

Kelli arrived at work an hour later. Beau and Dan were sitting at the bar discussing the menu. She hesitated by the door. She didn't want to intrude, yet it was partly her establishment, too. She approached them and Beau smiled when she got closer. "Just the person we were waiting for. Want

A Time To Heal · 101

to take a look at some menu changes Dan came up with?"

"Sure." She pursued the menu and saw new grilled items of shrimp and scallop skewers. "Looks good."

Dan nodded. "Quick and easy, plus in summertime, people want grilled."

Beau slapped him on the back. "Love it. You've got a good eye for this."

Kelli watched the interaction with interest. Beau didn't hand out praise often and only if it was well deserved. She agreed Dan had a flair for knowing what should and shouldn't be be on the menu.

"What's that smell? Is something burning?" Kelli glanced towards the kitchen.

"Nothing's cooking." Dan started for the kitchen. He pushed open the door to see smoke coming from the stove. He grabbed the fire extinguisher and opened the oven. Smoke rushed out, but there was no fire. He cleared the smoke, waving a towel in the air.

102 ·Emma Leigh Reed

"What the hell, Dan…you could have started a fire." Kelli was on his heels along with Beau.

"I'm telling you, I wasn't cooking, and the oven wasn't on when I went into the bar."

"Well, it certainly is on now, set higher than it should. What's that? Spilled oil in the bottom…another few minutes and the whole thing could have been in flames." She glanced around the kitchen. "Where is it?"

"Where is what?" Dan stepped right in front of her. "You want to accuse me of something?"

Beau stepped up and put an arm between them. "Knock it off."

"Damn it, Beau. We need to talk."

Dan took a step back, but his eyes never left Kelli's face. "Don't you be accusing me of anything unless you have proof."

"What do you think she is accusing you of?" Beau questioned. "Whatever it is between you two, get it settled. Doesn't look like there is any damage, but we need to get the smell of smoke out of here." Beau started for the door.

Dan waited until Beau left. "You think I've been drinking, right? And now I'm doing things to put the bar in danger?"

"Haven't you been? I saw you with a drink this morning outside." Kelli stood, hands on her hips, ready for the battle that she knew was about to ensue.

"Oh, my God. Seriously? I had iced coffee this morning. Glass is still in the sink if you feel the need to check. What is your problem?"

Kelli's finger poked his chest. "My problem is you. Don't drink at work. This is my life, too, and I'm not going to have you screwing with it." Kelli turned and started to the door. Glancing over her shoulder, "Clean it up in here, Dan, and I'm seriously keeping an eye on you."

He cursed as she left. Damn it, he knew she was right about the drinking, but he would never screw with the bar. He allowed his mind to become clouded with his desire for her and now she was pissed at something he didn't do. He didn't know how the oven got turned on or the oil got inside, but someone was messing with him and the bar. Who? He didn't have any enemies that he knew of. The only one around here that was questionable was Kelli's ex who kept showing up. There was something nagging at Dan about the whole situation and Beau needed to fill in some answers as to what the story was there. If her ex was going to screw with them, he was going to be prepared.

Dan spent the next hour washing everything down and getting rid of the smoke smell. The oven appeared to be in working condition without any problems. Whatever had happened hadn't damaged anything.

It was a Tuesday morning and although open, it was always their slow time. Dan searched out Beau in the office. "Got a minute?"

"Yeah. Come on in."

Dan shut the door behind him and settled into the chair. "I need some answers."

"To?"

A Time To Heal · 105

"What's the deal with Kelli and her ex?" Dan met Beau's eyes. "I'm not fishing, but I think if there is going to be trouble and her ex could be behind it, I want to know."

"You think Aaron got in the kitchen and caused the problem? Why would you think that?"

"Well, I didn't do it and someone had to turn the oven on to five hundred. Not to mention, oil was poured directly on the bottom of the oven. Come on. Who else do you know that has been hanging around and could cause a problem?"

Beau sat back in his chair. "I don't think Aaron would go that far. But I don't really know the guy. Kelli was married to him for six years. He ran around on her and when it came out, he decided he wanted a divorce. Kelli doesn't take marriage lightly and wanted to try and make it work, but Aaron was adamant he wanted out and so she gave him what he wanted. They've been divorced a while now. It was hard on Kel, but I think she's starting to move on."

Dan was stunned. "He screwed around on her? Who does that to their wife?"

Beau chuckled. "You know there are a lot of guys out there that do that. You and I, we're not like that so we can't fathom it, but some men are just jerks."

"Yeah, I know, still…I really figured she had left him."

Beau leaned forward. "You've treated her like she was Mia and taken your anger out on her. You haven't been fair to her, man. I don't know what is going on or what she thinks you did, but you both have each other pegged wrong."

Dan nodded. "Yeah, I guess so. Why didn't she say something?"

"Like you said something to her? Come on, you let her believe that you were being a jerk for no reason…well, not that you have really had a reason for treating her that way, but you know what I mean."

A Time To Heal · 107

"Damn. I don't think I can talk to her, though…she's pissed and it doesn't help that, well, never mind."

"Uh uh, spill it…doesn't help that what?"

"The first night her ex showed up, I went to her apartment to check on her because I knew she was upset. I had no plan, but when I got there, I kissed her. I don't know what the hell came over me. It just happened…" Dan looked down, ready for Beau to ream him out. He glanced up, hearing laughter. "Dude, really?"

"I knew it. You two have been avoiding each other." Beau sobered. "I'm not getting involved in this one. You need to find a way to fix it…or hell, just throw caution to the wind and call her out."

"Call her out?"

Beau grinned. "She didn't slap you across the face when you kissed her, right?"

"No."

"Then call her out, kiss her again…don't be afraid of her. She's a romantic at heart and even though she's been through hell and back, she doesn't really hate men. And if you tell her I said that, I will deny it. You're on your own on this one. But, man, just make a move one way or another."

Dan stood. "You are no help at all and this conversation never happened."

Laughter followed Dan as he headed back to the kitchen. He shook his head. Damn, he should have known better than to go to Beau. He was his best friend, but he was also close friends with Kelli. He prayed Beau would keep his mouth shut to her.

Kelli was at the bar when Dan walked by. The laughter that came from the office made her smile, and her smile widened to a full grin when she saw how uncomfortable Dan looked as he walked by, avoiding eye contact. She glanced down as her phone indicated a text message coming in. From Aaron again. He just wouldn't give up.

Still in town. Lunch?

She contemplated ignoring it and then quickly typed a response. *Not a chance. Go home and don't bother contacting me again.*

After she was sure it had sent, she shut the phone off and slid it into her pocket. She was going to have to get a new number if he didn't lay off. They had had some good times, but this past week he seemed to be more intrusive than anything and it was making her uncomfortable. She had never seen this side of him. The charm, yes, and she knew he used that to his full advantage when he wanted something. But apparently, when he realized his charm wasn't going to work this time, he moved into a different persona. She didn't like it.

How far would Aaron go? Was Dan right that he would mess with the business just because Kelli was finally setting boundaries with him? She shook her head, scoffing at the idea. Aaron was a lot of things, but that vindictive? She couldn't—wouldn't—believe he was like that. She still believed there was good in everyone until they proved her wrong.

Chapter Twelve

Kelli and Beau had been overwhelmed with the success of the bar. Today she could appreciate the bar being closed and having some down time. Everything was up and running, and the live music was a huge hit.

Beau had lent a helping hand when Kelli helped Jillian and Aiden move out of Kelli's apartment into a small place. Aiden had become a regular fixture around the bar, hanging out in the office during busy times and sitting in the dining

A Time To Heal · 111

room enjoying the music at slower times. He was well behaved.

Kelli was headed to Jillian's new place, walking and enjoying the gorgeous day.

"Hey, need a ride?" Beau's voice came from the vehicle beside her.

Kelli glanced at the truck. "In that rat trap? No, thanks. It's gorgeous out and I need the exercise, anyway."

"Need the exercise? Girl, you have been running more than anyone I know. Get in the vehicle."

Kelli sighed. "Whatever." She climbed in and turned to Beau. "I'm surprised you're headed to Jillian's. That is where you are going?"

"Yeah. She needed help with the beds. Dan and I are going to pick them up."

Kelli inhaled sharply. "Dan?"

"He's not all bad, you know. Besides, who can say no to Aiden?"

"Yeah, that's true. Aiden is a charmer." They rode in comfortable silence.

The town was small and Kelli loved the fact that she could walk to just about anything. The bar was located on the main highway, but right around the corner was Main Street, a quaint place with lines of local businesses and a coffee shop. Kelli's favorite place to browse was a small store that was a collection of books, antiques and knick-knacks. It was a tiny shop, but when she was there, it filled her with a homey feeling. It was a town where people knew everyone and talk about the newcomers lasted a few days. Apparently, after you had been in town for more than a month, you were no longer considered a newcomer but just one of the family.

Weekends were filled with people roaming the streets and shops, the town square filled with kids playing football, soccer or whatever game they had decided on. It was a town she wished she could raise a family in. Over the six years of her marriage, she had been pregnant once. An ectopic pregnancy. She had wanted a baby so badly. Aaron accused her of getting pregnant on purpose. She hadn't, but he wouldn't listen. Instead, being the heartless bastard he had been, he had told her he was glad the pregnancy hadn't come full term and was adamant about never wanting children. It had left an empty hole in her heart. A hole that had been shredded to encompass her whole heart when she found out he had fathered another child during their marriage, a child who was now three, being born shortly before she even found out about the affair.

It still caused a physical ache in her when she thought about her lost child and the thought of never having that with anyone else. She loved Aiden so much and doted on him whenever possible. He filled that ache a little bit. Jillian knew of the lost child and cried with Kelli numerous times over it. Only a mother could understand the intense pain of losing a child, even if it was during pregnancy.

Kelli pushed the thoughts aside as they pulled into Jillian's driveway. Aiden was sitting on the front steps waiting for them. "Aunt Kelli!"

Kelli pulled him into a fierce bear hug, kissing the top of his head. "How's my favorite kiddo?"

114 ·Emma Leigh Reed

"Great. Mom made muffins. Come on." Aiden's energetic nature was infectious and Beau and Kelli followed on his heels into the house.

Kelli stopped short when she came into the kitchen. Dan sat at the table, eating a muffin, smiling. She had never seen a smile on the man's face. His whole demeanor changed. The small laugh lines around his eyes made him more attractive. He was dressed in a tight fitting T-shirt that showed off his toned abs. Kelli swallowed hard and glanced at Jillian, who had a smirk on her face.

Kelli shook her head. "Ready to get this place in shape?"

"Just about. As soon as the men stop stuffing their faces, we can shoo them off to get the furniture."

Dan reached for another muffin as Beau buttered his. "If you weren't such a good cook, we would be out of here already." He grinned at her and Kelli found herself battling a flare of jealousy until she saw Jillian watching Beau. The look on her face was priceless and disappeared just as quickly.

A Time To Heal · 115

So they both were sporting crushes. Crushes? Where had that come from? Kelli tried to refocus on Aiden yet she couldn't seem to keep her eyes from wandering back to Dan.

Soon the men were ready to head out, deciding Aiden needed to go with them. Jillian and Kelli were left alone. Jillian picked up the kitchen, putting things away while Kelli sat at the table. "When were you going to tell me?"

"Tell you what?" Jillian turned to face her, leaning against the counter.

"That you think Beau is hot." The statement brought a flush to Jillian's face.

"What do you mean?"

"Oh, please. Don't be coy with me. It's all over your face when you look at him."

"Much like what is on your face when you look at Dan?"

Kelli shook her head. "Not a chance."

"Yup, okay. Let's get to work before they get back." Kelli was thankful she was given the brush off. She still hadn't come to grips herself with the feelings that bombarded her every time she was around Dan—the way her stomach fluttered when his eyes caught hers and wanting him to kiss her again.

The men returned after a couple of hours and they spent the rest of the day setting up the house with new furniture, painting the bathroom and getting rid of boxes. Jillian brought very little with them, just a couple of suitcases filled with clothes and the money she had been hiding—money that Kelli had been feeding her for the past four years, money that bought her furniture and small items that were needed. Kelli had picked up dishes and pots and pans at a thrift store for her.

"Finally feels like a home," Jillian said as she sank into the couch.

"Can we have pizza for dinner?" Aiden asked. The plight of an eight year old, always thinking of the next meal.

"Sure, my treat." Kelli spoke, seeing the fleeting look of panic cross Jillian's face, knowing money was tight.

A Time To Heal · 117

"I'll go pick a couple of them up," Beau spoke up.

"I'll go with you. We can stop at the store and pick up some drinks and chips, too," Dan chimed in.

"You guys have already done so much for us." Jillian was too tired to argue, but made a half-hearted attempt.

"You're family; besides, we can't let Aiden starve to death." She winked at the boy. "But I think we ought to get it fairly quick here before he collapses from exhaustion. I have a feeling he will be gone for the night when he goes down."

Within the next half hour, they were sitting on the floor of the living room munching away on pizza and chips. Jillian and Aiden were having a hard time keeping their eyes open when they all agreed it was time to give them some peace.

"Need a ride, Kel?" Beau helped her to her feet.

"Yeah, if you don't mind. I'm wiped out myself." She bent down and kissed Aiden. "Sweet dreams."

"Thanks for the help again, guys. I'll see you tomorrow." Jillian started to stand.

"Don't get up." Kelli gave her a quick hug.

Beau and Kelli climbed into the truck. She watched Dan walk across the lawn and up onto the porch next door. "He lives next door?"

Beau glanced at her while he turned on the truck. "Yeah. He owns the house Jillian is renting. You didn't know?"

"No."

She reached over and slapped Beau, who was laughing. "Puts a new perspective on Mr. Miserable, huh?" Beau said.

"Oh, shut up."

Chapter Thirteen

Kelli woke up to the sound of pouring rain on the roof Tuesday morning. It was dark and dreary. She rolled over and closed her eyes. The pounding rain kept her from going back to sleep. Six o'clock. She sighed and resigned herself to the fact that she was up whether or not she wanted to be.

Her coffee maker was set and ready. She pushed the on button and waited for the magical aroma to fill the air. Her body ached from painting yesterday. Jillian was settling in and she seemed more relaxed than Kelli ever remembered seeing her be. Aiden was adjusting well and looked forward to coming to the bar with Jillian at night. When it got real late, Kelli would take him upstairs to her place so he could settle down on the couch and watch a movie, usually falling asleep before Jillian was done work.

It was tough moving him at two a.m. every day back home to bed, but it was summertime and Aiden didn't seem to mind, sleeping through it. He was getting too heavy for Jillian to lift and carry downstairs. Kelli knew a babysitter would need to be found soon so Aiden could stay home while Jillian worked. Beau had been living in this town for over five years now; hopefully, he would have some leads for her. Kelli shook her head. She couldn't help but try and solve issues like this for Jillian. Jillian always seemed to let her, but she knew without a doubt there was going to come a day when Jillian would be strong enough to stand on her own two feet and wouldn't want the help.

Kelli poured her coffee. She closed her eyes, inhaling the aroma. Aaron had told her how foolish she was for enjoying her coffee this way. She shook her head and sank into the couch, curling her feet up under her. There was nothing like that first cup of coffee in the morning, especially on a cloudy, damp day.

She hadn't heard from Aaron in a couple of days and Kelli prayed he got the hint and had gone home. She needed to erase all reminders from her marriage with him. The more distance she gained from it, the more she realized how toxic it had been. As her mind wandered back through her life, she realized that she had always fallen for guys that had chipped away at her self-worth. Not one relationship had ever built her up, made her feel valued.

Kelli repeated the mantra that had become part of her morning routine. *I was worthy of friends. I deserved a decent life. I was a confident woman. I was a good businesswoman.* Although being completely out of her comfort zone, Kelli knew this move had been the best decision she had made in many years. Reconnecting with Beau brought her confidence to a new level. Beau never sugarcoated anything, but was always brutally honest with her. He also believed in her more than anyone ever had. Life was good.

Kelli spent the next few hours before work curled up with a good book, relaxing and enjoying her newfound freedom. Before she knew it, it was almost eleven and she was needed downstairs before the opening of the bar. Dashing through the driving rain, even the umbrella couldn't keep her dry.

Hopefully the rain would bring in customers for lunch. Tuesdays were notoriously slower than the rest of the week, although every night they seemed to have a steady crowd of regulars. She shook the rain from her clothes and hair.

"Umbrella didn't seem to help much. You're dripping," Beau stated.

"You think? What a storm."

A Time To Heal · 123

"Probably won't be too busy for the lunch crowd."

"Or the opposite. With the rain, no one is at the beach," Kelli countered. "A little positive thinking."

By one o'clock Kelli's prediction had come to fruition and there was a good crowd in the bar. Kelli was busy and enjoying the day despite the rain when Aaron walked through the door.

"What are you doing here? I thought you had gone back home."

"I'm here for lunch. And no, I'm not leaving until you and I can discuss things further." He gave her his charming smile.

"There is nothing for us to talk about, Aaron. Go home. You are not wanted here." Kelli turned and walked off, leaving him at the door.

"Kel, do you want me to seat the man at the door?" The young waitress, Jane, stopped her.

"Yes, that's fine." Kelli continued to the kitchen, not sure where she was going to go as she couldn't sneak outside with the downpour still going on.

Dan looked up as she came in, but was silent. She made her way to the coffee maker and poured herself a cup. She held her coffee and stared out the window above the coffee maker. The rain mesmerized her as she lost herself in what ifs. What if she did take him back? What if he treated her just as badly as before? What a fool she was to even entertain the idea. It wasn't what she wanted, but she couldn't stand up to him like she needed to. In some aspects, she still felt the need to walk on eggshells around him and say the right thing–whatever that might be in this situation.

"You okay?" She turned to find Dan standing beside her.

"Yeah. In this rain, no place to really get away. Sorry to invade your space again."

Dan poured himself a cup of coffee. "Ex back?"

"Yup." Kelli leaned her hip against the counter. "Why do you do that?"

"Do what?" Dan's eyes were quizzical.

She tore her eyes away from his. "You're a bastard most of the time towards me and then you have these moments where you actually seem to be sincere."

"It's not personal when I'm a jerk." He caught her gaze again. "Kelli…"

She tipped her head and watched him. "Yes?"

"I don't know…I just…" His words trailed off and he looked away.

"I should get back out there." She refilled her cup and hesitated as she watching Dan.

He refused to meet her eyes again. "Okay. Don't worry about having to come back here if you need to escape. I won't bother you about it."

She nodded and left the kitchen. He was an enigma. The soft side of him that he showed very rarely was such a turn on. Kelli wanted to see more of that man. Maybe Beau was right that he would come around in time.

Kelli went and stood behind the bar. At least the steady stream of people had slowed down to a trickle and the waitresses were handling patrons coming in and those waiting to be seated. Keeping an eye on Aaron without being obvious, Kelli wondered how she could get him to leave. He was insistent upon having a conversation. Well, maybe it was time to bite the bullet and just have it out with him.

Beau came up behind her from the office. "Looks like you were right. Good crowd because of the rain."

"You really need to learn to listen to me more often. I'm never wrong."

He snickered. "Keep telling yourself that."

She nodded in the direction of where Aaron was sitting. "He's back."

"Want me to throw him out?"

"On what grounds? I guess I need to just go talk to him and hopefully he will get it through his thick skull that we are through."

"I don't get why all of a sudden he wants you back. Don't get me wrong, you are a catch and he was an ass to let you go."

A Time To Heal · 127

"I know. He wanted the divorce and now he's sorry. I'm not buying it, either." Kelli shrugged. "He has to have something else up his sleeve, but for the life of me, I've no idea what it could be."

Kelli walked over to Aaron's table.

Kelli sat down across from Aaron. "Okay, what do you want to talk about?"

Aaron took a sip of his beer. "Have a drink with me."

"No, thanks. Look, Aaron, what do you want?" Kelli stared at him. "I don't have time for this and I want you to go home and leave me alone."

"Kel, I miss you. You can't blame me."

"Yeah, as a matter of fact, I can blame you. You didn't want to be married, remember? You didn't want to stay faithful to your wedding vows." Kelli exhaled slowly to control her temper.

"I know. I was wrong."

128 ·Emma Leigh Reed

"You were wrong? That's all you have to say?" Kelli stared at him.

"I never meant to hurt you."

"You're telling me that if I said yes, you could come back, you'd be a changed man?"

"Of course." Aaron played with his beer bottle and refused to meet her eyes.

"Liar." Kelli stood. "I'm done, Aaron. Leave me alone and go home. You'll never be a part of my life again. You had your chance and you blew it. Your choice, your decision, but you made it, not me. I simply gave you what you wanted."

Kelli didn't wait for an answer, but headed towards the bar. Aaron would never be satisfied with his life. He didn't know how to be a man and take responsibility for his actions. Kelli had had enough and for the first time since Aaron told her he wanted a divorce, she felt relieved and confident that walking away from the toxicity of their relationship was a good decision. Tension released from her shoulders in waves and relaxation overtook her. It hit Kelli how happy and content she finally was with her life.

Jillian dropped off empty bottles at the bar when Kelli slid onto a stool next to her. "You okay?"

Kelli nodded. "Absolutely. My eyes have been opened to the liar that he is."

"Hopefully he will get the hint and take off now."

Kelli glanced over her shoulder to see Aaron leaving The Salty Claw. "One can hope."

Kelli looked around. The crowd had dispensed when the rain stopped and now that the sun was out it had actually gotten quiet again. She grabbed a damp cloth, wiping down tables. Out of the corner of her eye, she saw Dan come out of the kitchen and head to the office. She continued with her task as her mind wandered to the side of Dan she saw yesterday at Jillian's. He was relaxed and enjoying himself. His eyes had seemed bluer as they sparkled with laughter at Aiden's antics.

There were times she liked her solitude of her life, but then, at other times, the loneliness overtook her and she missed having a man in her life. Since meeting Dan, she had been thinking more frequently of possibly wanting to give another man a chance. Could she learn to trust again after her failed marriage? Or would every man she tried to have a relationship with end up hurting her? Could she take the chance at love again? Kelli knew she was a romantic at heart, but she became a master at protecting herself. She came off as being cold-hearted at times, but it really was a defense mechanism. More than once she wondered if Dan's being a bastard was a protection of his heart. He had those moments of total sincerity that she found herself longing for.

"Kel?" Beau called out to her.

She glanced up and noticed him gesturing to her. "What's up?"

"Things have slowed down. If you want to take a few hours off before the night rush, go ahead."

"I wouldn't mind. You sure you don't need the help?"

"Nah, Jillian is here." Beau searched about the room looking for her.

"Yeah, okay. I'll see you later then." Kelli dropped her cloth into the soapy water and started for the door. A run would be just the thing to help clear her mind.

Chapter Fourteen

The Salty Claw was a success. The first month open had brought in great sales. Kelli knew that the busyness would drop off as the tourist season passed, but with another two months before that happened, she was counting on bringing in enough to carry them through the winter. Tourists loved the fact that it was so centrally located. Around the corner from Main Street, on the main throughway and across from the beach. It was the perfect

A Time To Heal · 133

location for it. The live bands on weekends also brought in a lot of their followers.

As time passed, Kelli became more and more relaxed. Beau and she were in sync with their thoughts of what was needed and how to go about making it happen. The only issue was the tension between Dan and herself.

Kelli swung open the office door. "Got a minute?"

"Of course. What's up?"

Kelli parked herself in the chair and drew up her knees. She wrapped her arms around her legs. "I've been thinking."

Beau chuckled. "Always a dangerous thing with you."

"Oh, shush. I've been looking into taking some online classes in business management. I wanted your opinion." Her old self had emerged, more confident and definitely happier.

Beau sat back, studying Kelli. "I think it's a good idea. You always wanted to finish school."

"I promise it won't interfere with my work here. They are all online, but I think I can do it."

"Kel, if you want to do it, then do it. We can work around your studying here. You've trained the staff so they know how to run things if you aren't here." He sat forward. "Do it."

Kelli broke into a grin. "I was hoping you would say that. I applied last night."

"Why ask me then if you didn't really want my answer?" Beau pretended to be offended.

"Oh, please. I knew your answer before I asked. I asked to make you feel special." She blew him a kiss as she headed for the door.

The hearty laughter that followed her into the bar put a spring in her step. She could always count on Beau to support whatever she wanted to do. It was a support that she never felt from her own family. Excitement and anticipation bubbled over. Kelli couldn't contain the giddiness she felt at the thought of doing all the things she had always wanted to accomplish and never had the courage to do.

A Time To Heal · 135

Life had smoothed out. She had not heard from Aaron since that day she told him they were done and there was no going back. What a relief. A huge weight lifted from her. She made the decision to not go backwards in her life and that made her confidence soar. Here was hoping he got the hint.

Kelli pulled out her sketch pad as she sat down at the bar. She had been working on a sketch for some outdoor seating for next year. Completely engrossed in adding in umbrellas to the tables, she started when Dan slid into the stool next to her.

"What's that?"

"Just some doodles." Kelli started to close the sketchbook, but Dan pulled it out of her hands, looking at each picture closely.

"These are good. Looking to expand?"

"Just some thoughts for next year. We could use the extra room and if we had outdoor seating, it would just give us that much more we could serve."

Dan slid the book back to her. "Nice. I didn't realize you were an artist, among your other talents."

136 ·Emma Leigh Reed

"Other talents?"

"Keeping Beau in line." He smiled briefly.

"Ahh, yes, my many talents. I always loved to draw, just never did a lot of it seriously. It was usually just doodling and put away somewhere." Kelli looked at the pictures she had drawn. She never saw them as good, more of a necessity to convey what her thoughts were.

"Keep at it. You really are talented." Dan stood. "Beau in the office?"

"Yup." She dismissed him, studying the doodles, trying so hard to see her pictures through Dan's eyes.

It would be a few weeks before classes started for her and she was excited, yet scared to death to venture out on this journey. Maybe she could sneak in a few art classes as electives for her business degree.

Chapter Fifteen

Dan took a long drink of his vodka and orange juice. One year...one year today that Mia had stormed out of the house and gone drinking. He had no idea what happened after that until the moment she hit his car. Dan spent his time coming to grips with giving her a divorce and then looking for her, only to have her be killed by her own stupidity.

Yet in the past year, Dan had come to the conclusion that Mia received the easier answer to their issues. Riddled with guilt, Dan spent the last year drinking, wishing he was the one that had died, and now with Kelli around, wondering why he couldn't allow himself to give into the feelings he had for her. Damn Mia. She still was controlling his life and he wanted her to let go. He wanted off this merry-go-round of guilt, wanting love, and guilt for that desire again.

He drained his glass and went to the kitchen to make another. He had to work in a couple of hours. He played with the idea of calling out sick, but he didn't want to let Beau down. He never gave it a thought that the drinking was going to impair his judgment on this. He filled his glass with ice and poured a shot of vodka before filling the glass with OJ.

His mind drifted to Kelli. How he didn't want to think of her tonight. Tonight he only wanted to curse Mia and his life that he thought was so good– a marriage that he wanted to work more than anything, to mourn the loss of their unborn child and the hope that they could try again. Instead, all that was torn from him with Mia's choice to hate him after the miscarriage, pulling away. The marriage had disintegrated and along with it, his ideal of what love should be.

He drained his drink in one swallow and placed the glass in the sink. He headed to the bedroom to change for work. He needed to get through this night and prayed Kelli would stay out of the kitchen. Right now it was all he could do to keep his hands off her. Maybe that's exactly what he needed to keep his mind of Mia. *No*! He needed the anger and the hatred right now, just for tonight. He deserved this one night on the anniversary where she ripped his life apart to mourn all that he lost and the fact that he had no control of the outcome. Damn, he wanted another drink.

The night started busy, for which Dan was thankful. He kept pushing through it and getting the meals out without drinking more than a glass of orange juice. When the break came in the orders, he couldn't keep himself busy enough. He poured a healthy dose of vodka into his orange juice from his stash in the kitchen. He called in the extra cook, stating it was busy and as it slowed, he told him to stay. He didn't want to jeopardize the kitchen and the quality of meals going out. Dan was thinking at least of the bar if he couldn't think of himself.

Dan continued his steady diet of orange juice and vodka. He tried to focus on the orders as the other cook finished them. He finally gave up and just leaned against the counter. Sulleness overtook his demeanor.

"Go home, man. I've got this."

Dan stared at the young man. He had called him in to work and now having the second chef there just irritated him. He wanted to be alone, but not in that house–the house he shared with Mia and all the memories that went with it.

"I'm not leaving. I've got this." Dan muttered. He put his drink down and jumped into work once again. There were only a few orders for the moment. He struggled to focus, finally succeeding in making his hands work with his brain, clearing the fog just enough to give the impression of being composed. He was tore between being thankful

A Time To Heal · 141

Kelli hadn't graced the kitchen all that much that night and being irritated that he hadn't seen her enough.

Kelli needed a breather. The bar had been busy tonight so far. It was only seven o'clock and there was a bit of a break. A cup of coffee should help.

"Jillian, watch the door, would you? I need to take a quick break and get a cup of coffee."

"Sure thing. Take your time." Jillian cleared off the table she was working on and handed Kelli the tray. "Drop these off in the kitchen for me?"

"You got it. Thanks." Kelli pushed the kitchen door open and dropped off the tray at the dishwasher before moving to the coffee maker. She reached for a mug and noticed a bottle of vodka from the corner of her eye. It was pushed behind a stack of plates, but it was almost empty. If it was the same bottle she had seen before, there was no way Dan had used that much for vodka sauce in a month, could he?

"Need help?" Kelli turned at the sound of Dan's voice. She found him smirking at her.

"Nope. I can pour my own coffee, thanks."

"Whatever. Hope you're not planning on holing up here." He turned and walked away.

What the...Kelli stared after him. He had seemed to soften over the past month and now tonight he was worse than when she first met him. She poured her coffee and took her time doctoring it up. She glanced over to his work station and there was a glass of orange juice. Was it doctored up with alcohol? She had no proof he was drinking, just a gut feeling.

She headed out to the bar and stopped at the door. "Thanks for the warm welcome back here." Dan stiffened before she turned and walked out. It was time for a chat with Beau.

Beau laughed with one of the customers at the bar. It was a knife in her heart to have to tell him Dan was drinking.

"Beau, can I steal you for a minute?" Kelli called to him from the end of the bar.

A Time To Heal · 143

"Sure." He turned to the customer. "Excuse me."

"Look, we need to talk. Have you seen Dan tonight?" Kelli sipped her coffee.

"Kelli, don't start on Dan tonight."

"Are you kidding me? Do you know what is going on?"

Beau sighed. "Yes. It's the one year anniversary of his wife's death."

"What? Why is he working then?"

Beau leaned on the bar. "You didn't know?"

"No. I didn't, but I think he's drinking in the kitchen."

"Come on, Kel. He may be an ass tonight, but do you think he would do that?"

"Seriously? You're going to be that naïve?" Kelli shook her head. "Beau, here's a reality check. Dan should not be working tonight and if you aren't going to do anything, I'm going in there and sending him home."

"I'm telling you, he should not be home alone tonight. Can you just cut him some slack?"

"Nope. This is my money invested here and I'm not taking the chance. He's gone tonight. You can tell him or I can."

Beau straightened. "Fine. I'll tell him, but you're coming with me because I want you to see you're wrong."

"Whatever."

They went into the kitchen. Dan leaned against the counter, drink in hand. "Whatcha drinking, Dan?" Beau stopped short in front of him.

"Orange shoosh. What elsh would it be?" Dan was belligerent with a slur to his words.

"Crap, Dan. Give me that." Beau grabbed the glass and took a sip. "You're done tonight. Pack it up. I'll call you a cab."

"I'm not leaving the kitchen. There's more orders to go out. I've got this." Dan fell back against the counter and pointed to Kelli. "This is her idea, isn't it?"

Kelli was beside him in a flash. Putting her arm around his back, she brought his arm around her shoulder. "Come on. You can go up to my place and sleep it off."

"How very Florence Nightingale of you." Dan leaned on her. Her free hand rested on his side, his muscles rock hard under her hand.

"Come on." Her voice was low and she shot Beau a look. "Have Jillian cover for me. I'll be back in a few."

"Need some help?"

"Nope, I've got this. If he falls down the stairs, he will deserve it." Kelli flashed a smile at Beau. "And no, I won't push him."

Dan walked beside Kelli, mumbling under his breath. She got him to the stairway up to her apartment and stopped. "You've got to help me out here, Dan. I can't pull you up these stairs. Come on, lift your feet."

They made their way up the flight of stairs. To Kelli, it took a lifetime. How much more could she take? The pain in his blue eyes spurred this decision.

146 ·Emma Leigh Reed

"It wasn't my fault." Dan leaned further onto her. She staggered under his weight.

"What wasn't?"

"The accident. I was going to look for her. How could she do this?" Dan fell through the door and Kelli tried to hold him up. They fell onto the couch with Kelli landing on top of him. His hands wrapped around her, holding her tight.

"She died. They said it was instant." He closed his eyes. Kelli pushed against him, trying to stand, but his arms tightened around her.

"I'm sorry."

"She'd been drinking. She hit me. Why didn't I die?" Dan's hand slid from her and Kelli stood. She stared down at him. His breathing evened into a deep slumber.

Shit. He was hit by his drunken wife. No wonder he couldn't cope. Kelli grabbed the blanket on the back of the couch and covered him. She lived with thoughts plaguing her of what she had done to cause Aaron to go elsewhere, even though she knew it was not her fault, but she couldn't imagine the

A Time To Heal · 147

pain Dan felt of not only becoming a widower, but knowing it was his wife's fault for the accident.

Tears running down her cheeks brought her back to the present and out of her daydreams. She could feel his pain. Never had she had such a connection to someone that was hurting. The hard façade eased in his sleep. She couldn't tear herself away. Kelli sank down and sat against the couch. Dan rolled to his side, his arm coming over her shoulder and around her. He sighed.

Kelli reached up, grabbing hold of his hand and held it. With closed eyes, silent tears coursed down her cheeks. She opened her eyes with the opening of her door. Beau walked in.

"Just checking on you. You okay?" Beau kneeled in front of her.

"Yeah. I'm taking the rest of the night, okay? Can you guys handle things?"

Beau nodded. "Jillian's got it under control. I'll check on you guys in the morning." He stood, turning to leave. "Kelli, thank you."

148 ·Emma Leigh Reed

"I didn't know." She lifted her other hand and rubbed Dan's arm. "How can he stand the pain?"

"It will get better. Maybe he'll tell you the whole story some day." Beau was gone.

Kelli turned and laid her head on the couch next to Dan, holding tightly to his hand. She watched him sleep. Would he accept her help? What could she do? She put herself in his position. Kelli was stubborn and would refuse help—much like Dan. They really were two of a kind.

Chapter Sixteen

Bright sunshine filled the room. Dan squinted as he glanced around. How much had he drank last night? He turned his head to see Kelli sitting on the floor with her head on the couch, sound asleep. Oh, his head hurt, but the sight of Kelli breathing softly next to him warmed him, lessening his pain.

He slowly eased his hand from hers. Standing slowly to not wake her, he went to the kitchenette. The least he could do was make her coffee before he left. Dan started the coffee maker. While he was waiting for it to brew, he splashed water on his face and dried it with a paper towel.

Dan turned to find Kelli watching him. "Good morning."

"Morning. How do you feel?" She stood slowly, stretching with arms overhead. Her shirt pulled tightly as she moved.

Dan muffled a groan and nodded. "Yup, fine. I started coffee."

"The smell woke me. My magic potion." She started down the hall. "Mugs in the cupboard above the coffee maker. Be right back."

Dan pulled out two mugs. He folded the blanket and put on the back of the couch. Kelli padded back into the room just as the machine beeped, announcing the coffee was ready, then poured both cups. "How do you take it?"

"Black for me. Thanks."

She doctored hers and handed him the other mug as she sank into the end of the couch. She crossed her legs. Automatically, she inhaled the aroma with her eyes closed. Kelli opened them with her first sip to find Dan smiling.

"What?"

Dan took a sip. "Do you always drink coffee through your nose?"

"Well, when you put it that way…no, well, yes. I mean…geez, haven't you ever smelled your coffee before you tasted it? The aroma just washes over you and then you can taste it more fully."

"I'll have to try it next time. Honestly, I have never seen anyone enjoy their first cup of coffee like you do."

Kelli giggled. "Yeah, well, I'm quirky that way."

"Quirky? Yup, that's one way of putting it."

Kelli raised her eyebrow and shook her head. "Are we going to dance around what happened last night or do you want to talk about it?"

"Didn't know we were dancing around it. I thought we were just making small talk first."

"Um hmmm. Want to tell me what last night was about?"

Dan shook his head no. "Really? Beau hasn't filled you in?"

"I learned more last night from you than Beau ever told me. You know he's a loyal friend. He'd never betray any confidence."

"Yeah, I know. I don't know what I said. Honestly, I don't remember most of last night, including how I got up here."

"Well, that was the fun part. You weren't very cooperative coming up the stairs, but I had promised Beau not to push you down them, so we made it."

"How gallant of you. Thank you for restraining yourself, though I would have deserved that push."

"Ain't that the truth?" Kelli continued sipping her coffee, waiting for him to give her a real answer.

Dan drank his brew. He set the mug on the end table and turned to face Kelli. "I don't even know where to start. I was in a car accident a year ago. My wife, Mia, was the driver of the other car."

"And she was drinking, right?"

A Time To Heal · 153

Dan nodded. He met Kelli's eyes. The pain intensified the blue in his eyes, tearing through her. "We had had a fight and she left. While I waited for her, I came to the conclusion that the marriage was over. I didn't know she was out drinking...I didn't know where she was. In my mind, I guess I thought she was having an affair, but I will never know."

Kelli silently took it in. Dan closed his eyes, gathering his thoughts. "I guess that's the worst part. I will never know. There's no closure to it, not like a divorce."

"You think that there is closure with a divorce? At least you can grieve and it is acceptable." Kelli took a deep breath. "No one understands that even with a divorce you are grieving a loss, but there's no closure."

"True, but at least you have answers."

Kelli shook her head. "No, not really." She stood and grabbed his coffee cup. "Another one?"

"Sure."

Neither spoke while she poured more coffee for them. She stirred in cream and sugar into hers and made her way back to the couch. "You've been through a tough ordeal, but you can't let it decide your life."

"Words of wisdom from the one whose ex wants her back."

"You think I don't feel guilty that I couldn't make my marriage work or that my husband chose to betray our wedding vows? Trust me, in the past couple of years, there isn't a day that I don't wish there had been a death instead. It would be better than the alternative."

"What's the alternative?"

"Rejection."

Kelli met his eyes and melted. The pain had lifted. They were bluer than ever, if that was possible, glistening with unshed tears. Her heart sped up, beating loudly. Could he hear it? She ran her tongue over her lips and wished he would kiss her.

"Kelli, I probably should go." Dan set his coffee down.

A Time To Heal · 155

"Don't go." She whispered the words. She reached behind her and placed her coffee mug on the other end table. She waited, watching him.

"This probably isn't a good idea."

"Because it's a bad idea? Or because you're scared?" She bit her bottom lip. "I'm afraid to let anyone else in, too."

Dan didn't say a word, but reached for her hand. He pulled her close to him, bringing his other hand to her face. "I don't want to hurt you."

"Then don't. There are no expectations...I just want you." Kelli leaned forward and Dan met her, his lips caressing hers with a gentleness she had never experienced. She ran her hand around his neck, pulling him closer.

Dan's hand slid along her hip, up to the edge of her shirt. He hesitated for a brief second before raising her shirt slowly, his hands resting on her ribs. He pushed her back against the couch and lay down beside her. His leg settled between her thighs and she pulled him closer. The kiss broke off and they searched each other's eyes. Kelli's hand slid to his chest, her fingers bringing his shirt into her fist.

A knock on the door brought Dan up off the couch with a groan, his hand reaching for Kelli and pulling her to a sitting position. She straightened her shirt as she stood to answer the door. She glanced back to see Dan sitting on the couch, coffee mug in hand finishing his coffee.

Kelli swung open the door to find Beau standing there. "Hope I'm not waking you."

"Of course not. Come on in. Coffee?" Kelli moved to the kitchenette.

"If it's all made, sure." Beau made himself comfortable and glanced between Kelli and Dan. "Did I interrupt something?"

"No. I was just getting ready to leave." Dan took his mug to the sink. "Thanks, Kelli, for the place to crash last night."

"No problem. Take the day off if you want." She handed Beau his cup.

"No. I'll be at work tonight, sober."

"Good to know. You won't be working at all if you have had just one drink." Kelli smiled sweetly.

"Got it. See you later, Beau."

Kelli felt a stab of disappointment as Dan closed the door behind him. How far would it have gone if Beau hadn't shown up? She wanted Dan. Yes, she could finally admit it. He had wormed his way into her heart and she felt he was a kindred soul.

Chapter Seventeen

Kelli rinsed her coffee cup, keeping her back to Beau. Breathing in deeply, she exhaled slowly.

"I did interrupt, didn't I?"

Kelli turned at the words. "Of course not. Nothing to interrupt."

Beau sipped his coffee. "Whatever you say."

"He needed a place to crash, that was it." Kelli slipped onto the couch. "You never told me his wife was the one that hit him."

"Yeah. It wasn't my story to tell."

"You preferred I was blindsided with that information. I told you at the beginning, I needed to know things."

"Come on, Kel. It wasn't necessary you know that information when you first got here." Beau raised his hand as she started to protest. "You didn't. I know you think you did, but it was Dan's story to tell."

"I know." Kelli was thoughtful. "How has he done it? I can't imagine losing my spouse in that type of situation."

"He gets up each morning and keeps going until it becomes easier. Just like you have done since Aaron left you." Beau stood and took his mug to the kitchen. "I'll see you later. Don't overthink his situation. It's really not that different from yours."

Kelli hugged Beau before he left. Shutting the door behind him, she leaned back against the door. Her mind whirled with the knowledge of Dan's tragic past. It was impossible to imagine how she would react if it had been her. To not have closure was a painful thing to deal with. She ached with how brokenhearted Dan was. She slid to the floor and pulled her legs up close, hugging them. Tears coursed down her cheeks as she silently grieved Dan's loss…a wife, a marriage and his hope for a future along with her own grief of her failed marriage and her dreams of a secured life with a partner that loved her more than anything. She cried until there were no more tears.

For the first time in a couple of years, she allowed herself to cry for all the disappointments she had experienced. She inhaled deeply and wiped her face. She leaned her head back against the door. This was going to be a tough situation. She wanted to know Dan better now…to know what made him tick. Those eyes killed her—they sucked her in and she melted inside. She was always a sucker for blue eyes, but his were an ocean blue, light and full of emotion. They showed his pain, yet sparkled when he laughed…they were the path to his soul. But the drinking…it was the cornerstone of the barrier between them.

How did she get to this place? In a position where she actually wanted more from a man? The thought of being able to have that type of intimate relationship with a man again scared her to death. Maybe she really wasn't ready for that. With a sigh, she stood up and headed for the shower. Work would be interesting today, to say the least.

The hot water rained over her. Kelli closed her eyes, allowing herself to think about the way Dan touched her this morning...the warmth his kiss spread throughout her. She shivered and shut off the water. Kelli berated herself for wanting him that much. Was she that sex crazed that she wanted any man that came into her life? She needed to keep her distance. He had been vulnerable and she shouldn't take advantage of that.

After dressing, Kelli applied a bit of mascara and looked at herself in the mirror. The mascara brought attention to her eyes. *What am I doing?* She shook her head, but left the makeup on and started down to the bar. She needed to speak with Jillian about Aiden and the need to find a babysitter for him. He couldn't keep coming to the bar every night with her. Kelli closed her eyes and willed herself to put Dan out of her mind. She needed to focus on something else and Aiden was it.

Kelli slipped in the front door of the bar and turned the open sign on. With any luck, it would be busy tonight, keeping her focused on the business and her mind off those incredible kisses from Dan this morning. *Damn, focus girl.*

Kelli walked around the bar, double checking tables and the bar area to make sure everything was ready for opening. Jillian walked in.

"Hey, thought you were working tonight?" Kelli pulled Aiden into a bear hug.

"Yeah, but I switched with Deb. I'm meeting with the older lady across the street from me around six tonight about her watching Aiden for me in the evenings."

"Oh, well that will be good. I was just thinking that you would need to start contemplating that."

Jillian laid a hand on Kelli's arm. "I know you mean well, but I've got this. I was strong enough to

A Time To Heal · 163

leave, I can do this. But thank you for always being there."

Kelli hugged her. "I know. I'll back off. I just don't want you to be overwhelmed. It took a lot to leave Sam."

"Love you, girlfriend, and I appreciate all you do for me and Aiden." Jillian squeezed her tight before stepping back. "I'm going to just check things in the kitchen."

"Go ahead." Kelli turned towards the hostess station and ignored the burning need to see Dan.

Chapter Eighteen

Kelli started for the office to check in with Beau. She stopped short when she heard Dan's voice. "I'm telling you, someone has been screwing with stuff in the kitchen."

"What do you mean?"

"Boxes that had been placed outside the door are moved. I had a new delivery of veggies and half of them were destroyed. Who's messing with things?" Frustration laced Dan's words.

A Time To Heal · 165

"I don't know, but we need to find out. Where were the veggies?"

"I had gone back inside to grab a few things. I left them right outside the door to bring in. I was only gone a total of ten minutes tops."

There was silence and Kelli leaned toward the door, not wanting to interrupt yet. "I had a case of wine get smashed, also. It was outside while I was hauling in other cases."

Kelli pushed open the office door. "Hey, what's going on?" She tried to be nonchalant and kept her eyes averted from Dan.

Beau glanced at Dan. "Appears we have someone playing some mischief with the bar. I guess I'll call Phil and see what he can do." Phil was the local chief of police and Kelli knew if Beau thought he needed to be involved, then he was worried.

"What kind of things? Kid stuff?" Kelli questioned.

"Broken bottles of wine, destroyed food." Beau looked at Kelli thoughtfully.

166 ·Emma Leigh Reed

Kelli shook her head. She knew what he was thinking, but Jillian's boyfriend didn't know where she was. He couldn't. "Do you think my flat tires and broken windows are related?"

Beau shrugged. "Not sure. The police never came up with anything."

Dan stood and headed for the door. "Let me know. I'm trying to keep a close eye on things, and I don't think it's staff. Why would they?"

Kelli sighed a breath of relief when Dan left the room. His silence caused an iciness to slice through her and she wanted the Dan that brought a warmth to her. She frowned as Beau completed his phone call to Phil.

"We'll get to the bottom of it, don't worry." Beau sat back and watched Kelli.

"I know what you're thinking and Sam doesn't know where Jill is."

Beau nodded. "I know you think that, but what if he does? Would he try to take out his anger on the bar? We have to think about it, Kel."

"I know, but it would kill Jillian if she thought she brought trouble here to us."

"I'm not blaming her, but if he is behind this, we need to catch him and stop him."

"But there were things that were happening before Jillian got here." Kelli closed her eyes. What a morning already and she wasn't sure she was up to dealing with all this. She really thought once Aaron left her stress level would decrease. Instead, she allowed herself to open her heart just a bit and Dan had somehow slid into that tiny crack, and now someone was trying to mess with the bar, stressing her out again.

"You okay?" Beau's voice broke through her momentary self-pity party.

"Yeah. The bar is doing so well, I can't stand the thought of something going wrong."

"You know things have a way of working out. Let's see what Phil says. He's coming over to look around."

Kelli nodded and headed out front. They were now open for the day and she wanted to feel like she was doing something instead of worrying.

The rest of the day flew by. Phil found nothing out of the ordinary, but as he said, there were so many people in and out, it would be hard to find footprints or the like around the kitchen. They decided they would have at least two people around for each delivery so nothing was left unattended. Irritation stabbed at Kelli for having to change their routine to accommodate some sicko who wouldn't leave them alone.

Beau and Kelli decided not to say much to Jillian in case it really was Sam. They didn't want to worry her if it wasn't necessary. They didn't want her running away again with Aiden. Besides, they could protect her if she was close. Kelli always adored Aiden, but he had wormed his way into Beau's and Dan's hearts, too. That little boy made everyone love him. They were going to miss not having him here at the bar every night, but they knew it was for the best.

A Time To Heal · 169

Dan stayed busy in the kitchen, doing his best to avoid Kelli. Although it certainly felt like she was avoiding him, too, he felt like an ass for not talking to her. If Beau hadn't showed up this morning, things would have gone much further. Dan wanted Kelli more than anything, more than he had ever wanted Mia. They had more of a connection than he had ever felt with anyone. He was petrified to allow her into his heart.

With the kitchen cleaned, Dan longed to see Kelli, to hold her. He had been a jerk this morning and ignored her in Beau's office, but he couldn't stand the thought of going home without talking to her. He walked into the main bar and noticed Beau and Jillian talking.

Dan smiled at the look on Beau's face. He obviously had it bad for her. "All set for the night?" Dan approached the two.

Beau turned towards him. "Yeah. All closed up. Kitchen locked up?"

"Yeah." Dan looked around.

"She already left for the night," Jillian offered.

Dan nodded, trying to hide his embarassement knowing he had been caught looking for Kelli. "See you tomorrow. Need a ride, Jillian?"

"Nah, I'm all set. Thanks, though."

Dan headed for the door. He stepped out into the cool air and paused to watch the ocean. He looked up at the apartment overhead and stared at the lit window. With a sigh, he turned towards his car. He couldn't. He wanted to, but he had to give himself some time. He needed to forget Mia. He berated himself all the way home, wishing he was holding Kelli tonight instead of entering an empty house that suffocated him every night, causing him to drink. A need he wanted to ignore since meeting Kelli.

Dan crossed the street and started walking down the beach. The ocean breeze mingled with the salty scent eased the pain in him. He walked to clear his head, yet his thoughts drifted to Kelli laying in bed. He could picture her curves, and the memory of running his hands over her shook his resolve to

A Time To Heal · 171

stay away. He found himself at the rocky cove and sat down. He let his head fall into his hands as tears formed in his eyes. His life was a mess and he had no control over anything anymore. He struggled to hold back the emotions that flooded him, crashing over him like the waves over the rocks just ahead of him.

He wanted Kelli and he couldn't have her. He wanted peace, and it eluded him. He wanted…He sighed. He didn't know what he wanted anymore or what he deserved to have.

Chapter Nineteen

He sat across the street in a dark sedan. They had closed up the bar and everyone was leaving. The last two, the owner and one of the waitresses, left together laughing. He scowled and waited until everyone was gone. The light went off in the apartment above the bar.

He got out of the car and crossed the street. At three in the morning there was no traffic and all was quiet. He made his way behind the bar to the kitchen door. It was locked tight and everything was picked up around it. The boxes that had been there the other day were broken down and now in the Dumpster. He searched around and came up empty.

Using his elbow, he broke the window in the kitchen and reached in to unlock it. He opened the door and looked around. In the dim moonlight, he moved about checking it all out. He didn't want to completely destroy it, but damn it, this could not be a success. She had never been successful and she wasn't going to start now.

He smashed plates, making sure there would be none left for service tomorrow. With each plate that hit the floor, his anger grew inside him. Looking around at the mess, he took a deep breath. That should teach her a lesson. With a grin on his face he left, confident he would be able to shut them down, at least temporarily, and by then she would know she couldn't do this and return to him.

Kelli woke to seagulls calling for breakfast. She still hadn't mastered the art of sleeping in. She glanced at the clock and seeing 7:00, she groaned.

Four hours of sleep. She rolled over, but within minutes knew she was not going to get any more sleep. A run would be the thing to truly wake her up and she flung back the covers to get up and start the day.

Crossing the street, Kelli stretched out on the beach and started down near the water towards the rocky area where she hoped Dan would be. Although she knew it was too early, she still hoped that he couldn't sleep, either, and would seek out this spot. Her feet pounded on the sand and with each step she felt her mood darken. The more her thoughts circled around how she would've given herself to Dan yesterday, the more irritated she got.

Yet deep inside, she felt ready. Ready to move on from mourning her marriage and all the mistakes she had made. She still held hope that there was someone out there that could love her. She was a hopeless romantic, which just fueled the irritation growing in her. The rocks were empty and she glared at the area that had become the shared spot for her and Dan. She continued down to the peninsular running trail. Yet again, Dan kept a firm spot in her mind and no matter how fast she ran, she couldn't clear him from her thoughts. She stopped, bending over to alleviate the pain stabbing her side. She gasped for air, forcing her breaths to be deep and slow.

The pain eased and she slowly straightened. She started the walk back, and moving at a casual walk, to work out the lingering ache in her side. Why couldn't she outrun the pain in her heart? She needed to let go of the past, but it was hard for her to have faith that life could get better. Kelli watched the ocean as she walked. The waves came in over and over again without fail. They washed over her mentally and slowly pushed away her self-doubts. Dan maybe was the key to moving on. Even if nothing developed between them, at least talking with him was therapeutic for her and she hoped for him, too. It was time to let the crack in her heart widen.

With renewed motivation and hope in her heart, Kelli started jogging the rest of the way home. She crossed the street to see Phil's police car and Beau at the corner of the bar. Kelli sprinted over.

"What's going on?"

Phil turned to her. "Did you hear anything last night after you went to bed, anything unusual?"

Kelli shook her head. "No. I fell asleep. What happened?"

Beau stepped closer to her. "Kitchen was broken into. All the dishes have been broken. I don't know if we can open today."

"No." Kelli looked from Phil to Beau. "You're going to let whoever did this win? No, I'll go shower and change, and then head over to the store. I'll buy out all the paper plates they have. We'll still open."

"That might work for a day, Kel, but we can't keep putting money out like that."

"We can replace the dishes. It will set us back a bit, I understand, but I'm not shutting down for some jerk." She turned towards Phil. "Any ideas who did this?"

A Time To Heal · 177

"No, but we'll find out." Phil shook Beau's hand, promising to call him with any news.

They watched Phil drive away. Beau turned and faced Kelli. "I called Dan to come help clean up. Go change and get those paper plates. I'll call our distributor and see if we can get more plates delivered ASAP."

Kelli nodded. She headed for her apartment as Dan drove in. She hesitated as he exited his vehicle. He never glanced at her. Beau started talking to him and the two men moved towards the kitchen. Kelli sighed and kicked herself into gear. Who was out to get them?

By the time Kelli had changed and gone to the store, Beau and Dan had the kitchen back in order. She walked in with a box filled with paper plates. "There's two more boxes in the car."

"I'll get them." Beau leaned his broom against the counter.

"Looks like nothing happened in here." Kelli set down the box.

178 ·Emma Leigh Reed

"It was a mess." Dan turned away, not making eye contact. "Hopefully you got enough plates."

"Well, Edna at the store said they had more, so just give her a call if we need them and they would get them to us immediately. I think we'll be okay at least for tonight."

"Good." Dan faced her, searched her. "Look…"

"Where do you want these?" Beau brought in the other two boxes, his vision clearly obstructed.

Dan grabbed one of the boxes. "Right here. I'll unpack them."

Kelli left the kitchen without a backward glance. Starting a sentence with "look" was not a conversation she wanted to have right now. She couldn't bear the thought of being rejected once again.

Chapter Twenty

The bar opened as normal. He waited for them to close and was furious when it filled up and was quite busy for the night. How could they have stayed open? He slammed his fist against the steering wheel. Damn it. He would need to step it up a notch. He could not let her ruin her life here. He didn't want her out like this, flaunting around a bar. His woman would not be acting like that.

He hadn't planned on spending another sleepless night to shut down this place. He wanted it over today. He started the car and drove off. He would have to come back after close. He had seen the police car cruising by a few times today, and knew it would be around tonight.

Dan's irritation at using the paper plates was obvious to Kelli. His dishes deserved more than this kind of presentation. She winced at the thought of going a few days like this. Beau had contacted the distributor and they were going to try and get new dishes here by tomorrow, but none of them were confident it would happen. Kelli had been in and out of the kitchen a few times and each time Dan had made sure he was too busy to talk to her. He had been an ass. She deserved better than this.

Jillian approached Kelli at the hostess station. "So what's the deal, girlie?"

Kelli raised an eyebrow. "Meaning?"

"Dan is in a foul mood in the kitchen. What's that about?"

A Time To Heal · 181

Kelli smirked. "And you assumed I had something to do with it or would know why? No idea."

Kelli could feel Jillian's eyes watching her as she seated more customers. "Don't you have work to do?" Kelli returned, marking off the seating chart.

"Sure, but it's not nearly as interesting as what's been happening with you two."

Kelli placed a hand on her hip. "Okay, who says something has happened? Geez, the man can barely stand me to begin with, let alone actually want to spend time with me."

"And that says it all right there." Jillian gave her friend a hug. "He'll come around. Don't give up on him."

"What are you talking about?" Kelli called after Jillian.

Kelli shook her head. She didn't know what Dan was saying or doing, but it would never do to have everyone think there was something between them. Kelli set her pen aside and started for the kitchen. She pushed through the swinging door and hesitated when her eyes met Dan's.

Dan nodded his head towards the coffee maker. "Coffee's fresh."

"Thanks." Not really in the mood for a cup of coffee, Kelli didn't have any other excuse for being in the kitchen so she proceeded to pour herself a mug.

"Kel…"

Kelli turned and leaned against the counter to find Dan just a step away. "Yeah?"

"I just…" He turned toward the door as Jillian came walking in.

"Order." Jillian placed the slip on the counter. She glanced between Dan and Kelli.

"Got it." Dan grabbed the slip and dismissed both of them.

Kelli shot a look of exasperation at Jillian as she walked past. Jillian fell in behind her. "I didn't mean to interrupt."

"You didn't."

A Time To Heal · 183

Jillian grabbed her arm so Kelli would look at her. "Really? Then why are you irritated with me?"

"Oh, stop…get back to work." Kelli sat down on a bar stool and sipped her coffee.

Beau wiped the bar down and stopped when he got in front of her. "No word from Phil yet. What are your thoughts on all this?"

Kelli tilted her head at him. "I have no idea. I highly doubt it's Sam, but who would want to cause problems here?"

"Aaron?"

"Come on, Beau. You don't really think Aaron would do this. Besides, I haven't heard from him since I made it perfectly clear we were done. As far as I know, he's long gone back home."

Beau shrugged. "Maybe. I just can't wrap my head around who would do this."

Kelli played with the mug. "Do you have any issues with anyone?"

Beau's chuckle was music to her ears. "Not likely."

"Well, it's either someone related to one of the staff, a band member or just someone completely loony. That leaves the options wide open, doesn't it?"

"Pretty much. Guess we'll wait until we hear from Phil. I'm concerned about you staying here alone at night though."

"I'm upstairs, doors are locked. Who's going to bother me?"

Beau leaned on the bar. "Kel, we don't know who it is. If they are just out for mischief of some sort, you could be in danger if they escalate."

"I guess, but I'm not leaving. This is my home now and I'm not being scared away."

"You are too stubborn for your own good. Please think about staying with Jillian for a couple of nights or you can stay with me…or maybe Dan wouldn't mind."

Kelli stood. "Enough. I'll consider staying at Jillian's. As far as the other idiotic suggestions you just made, I'm going to forget I heard them."

A Time To Heal · 185

The whole day was just irritating Kelli. From the break in and vandalism to everyone laughing at her expense. She just wanted to smack them all and be done with it. The rest of the night flew by. After closing, when everything was cleaned up, Beau gathered the staff that had been working.

"We need everything checked and double checked before leaving tonight. The window has been boarded up in the kitchen, but we want to make sure there is nothing else that would be enticing for someone to try and get in."

They checked everything and gathered their stuff before leaving. Jillian walked out with the other staff, leaving Dan, Beau and Kelli inside.

"What's the plan for tonight?" Dan asked.

Beau was silent for a few minutes. "I've debated if someone should stay here…and by that I mean me."

"That's ridiculous," Kelli snapped. "You won't get any sleep and if someone does get in, what do you think you're going to do? It's not a smart move."

"And it's not a smart move for you to stay upstairs by yourself," Beau shot back.

Kelli shook her head. "I'm not changing my life, but you need to go home." She started for the door. "I'm going home."

"God, that woman is stubborn." Beau grabbed his keys. "I'll call Phil on the way home and make sure they are doing checks on the building through the night."

Chapter Twenty-One

Kelli sat in the darkened apartment. Sleep would elude her tonight. She was exhausted and now with the break in-- she would never admit it to Beau-- but she was anxious about being here alone. She had to face this and not run, but what if someone did try to get into her apartment? She had her phone within reach and she was snuggled down on the couch with a blanket.

Kelli's small air conditioner was blowing on her and she snuggled deeper into the cover. She was so engrossed in listening for anything out of the ordinary she jumped a mile at the sound of a knock at the door. Kelli stood and tried to see through the window at who might be on her stairs. She couldn't see anything.

She punched in 9-1-1 into the phone and had her thumb poised over Send when she opened the door. Dan stood there.

"Damn it. You scared me. What are you doing here?"

"I was checking on you." He leaned against the doorframe. "Going to invite me in?"

"No." Kelli closed the door just a fraction and stood in the small opening. "Why are you here?"

"I told you. Beau thinks you're stubborn, and well, so do I."

"I'm not going anywhere and I don't need a bodyguard." Hearing the words come out of her mouth, Kelli wanted to take them back. She wanted him here with her, but he obviously wasn't ready for that. He had been avoiding her at all costs the last few days.

"Okay. I'll leave. At least I know you're okay and no one is around, from what I can see downstairs."

Kelli nodded. She swallowed hard and leaned her head against the door. Unconsciously, she ran her tongue along her bottom lip. She became aware of what she was doing when Dan's eyes dropped to her lips and watched her. He never blinked and when he lifted his eyes to meet hers, warmth spread over her face.

"I should go." Dan straightened, but made no move to turn towards the stairs.

"Mm hmm."

Dan reached out and entwined his fingers with the hair at the base of her neck. Pulling her towards him, he gently kissed her lips. She parted hers and sighed, leaning into him. It was all the encouragement he needed. His tongue sought hers out and stroked it. Her fingers hooked into his belt loops, bringing them even closer. His free hand slid down her back, coming to rest just below her waist. He pressed against her.

Kelli broke off the kiss finally. With her forehead against his, she closed her eyes. Dan's hand that had been holding her neck ran down her back and stop at her waist. She opened her eyes and watched him. His breathing was deep and he stood there with his eyes closed. Her thumbs made small circles on his waist just above his jeans.

Dan grabbed her hands and stilled her thumbs. "If I'm leaving now, you should stop that." His voice was quiet. She pulled her hands away from him and stepped back. Did she want him to stay or was it best if he left now?

She looked up and saw him watching her. She swallowed and stepped back again, leaving room if he wanted to step in. It was going to have to be his choice. She saw conflict flicker in his eyes. It was all she needed to see. "I'll see you tomorrow, Dan."

Those words tore through her. She would kick herself later, but didn't want any regrets if anything happened between them, on either side. He nodded and started downstairs without a word. Kelli shut the door and clicked the lock into place. It was going to be a long night indeed. Walking softly down the hall, Kelli's frustration grew. She ached with need for Dan, but knew it wasn't an issue she could push. He had to work through the conflict of his past himself. She understood all to much having to work through past issues and wondered sometimes if she had fully worked through her own.

Dan drove home, the radio playing softly in the background. A love song of heartache played and he questioned his actions. He wanted Kelli, but was he over Mia? He missed Mia, but not the marriage. Without realizing it, Dan drove right by his house. He continued to drive for the next hour not knowing where he was going or what he was hoping to find. The sky lightened with streaks of pink as the morning sun started to rise. He was fully aware that until Kelli and he hashed this out, he wouldn't be sleeping anytime soon. He turned his vehicle towards the cemetery and as the sun broke the horizon, he pulled up and parked next to Mia's grave.

Dan sat in the car, his hands on the wheel. He hadn't been here since the funeral. Over the past year, he knew he should've come and brought flowers or visited at least, but Dan never could bring himself to do that. Mia's mother had questioned him once why he never went to visit his wife's grave. He was elusive and fought to keep the truth from them. Their marriage had been a sham, not what her family thought it was. He wished for an instant he had a drink with him to give him the courage he needed.

Dan got out of the car and knelt beside the grave. He cleared dead flowers from in front of the headstone. Mia's mother had kept the stone clear of long grass and had a beautiful planter next to it filled with a small rose bush – Mia's favorite. Time ticked by as he sat in front of the grave, his mind spinning. Why was he really here? He cleared his throat and tried to form the words.

"We were supposed to be forever. I don't know what happened or whose fault it is, but I will take full responsibility. I pushed you to marry me when I

A Time To Heal · 193

found out you were pregnant. I shouldn't have. Did you feel you had no out? No options? God, I'm sorry, Mia." He ran his hand over his face. "Sorry for the way our lives ended up, for you running out. Was there someone else? I guess I will never know. For me, now there is. I want to move on and allow myself to feel again. Feel beyond this mind-wrenching numbness. I want to love again. I want to be loved." Dan stood. "Mia, a part of me will always love you, but I have to let go and move on. I hope you can understand that." He slid into his car and started it. This would be the last visit he would make here. It was time. Peace settled about his shoulders and the ache lessened in his heart.

Chapter Twenty-Two

Kelli willed her coffee to yield its magic and pull her from this fogginess surrounding her. All had been quiet around the bar the past few days. Phil had upped patrols through the night and so far nothing else had happened. Unfortunately though, that also meant that Phil had not come up with any answers as to who was behind the vandalism, her car and the bar.

Kelli pulled up her email and started going through it. She had ignored it the past few weeks

A Time To Heal · 195

and knew she was in for an onslaught of emails that needed to be answered. She waded through the junk emails and a couple of emails from friends. She would answer those later when she was more awake. The last few were emails from the college she had applied to. Acceptance email, next-steps email from her advisor…it was all happening. She read through her advisor's email twice and hit reply. Kelli filled her coffee cup again before typing a response to the next step and picking classes. Whether it was the coffee or the excitement of a new adventure starting in her life, she suddenly was wide awake and ready to go. Her advisor must have been online as she had a response immediately. She read through the list of options for her first classes and replied with her choices. Classes would start online in two weeks.

Kelli sat back and sipped the rest of her magical brew. This is what she needed to get her mind off Dan. His kisses were intoxicating and addictive. Never had she been with a man where she just craved his touch or his kisses long after he was gone. There was something about him and it was more than the loneliness and pain that filled his eyes, it was a connection between the souls with them. Maybe she was nuts. Who believed in soulmates, anymore? That was a thought for starry-eyed teenagers, not a young woman in her twenties that had lived through a disastrous marriage and a cheating husband.

She placed her mug in the sink. What she needed was some time with Jillian and Aiden—some much needed girl talk, and laughter with her favorite eight year old "nephew". Once in the car, she turned towards Jillian's. A knot formed in her stomach. Jillian lived next door to Dan. Hopefully, she wouldn't run into him. Today needed to be a Dan-free day. No thoughts of him and definitely no seeing those gorgeous blue eyes.

Kelli pulled into Jillian's driveway just as Beau was coming out the door. She parked to the side of Beau's truck. "Should I ask?" Kelli asked as she exited the vehicle.

"Just stopped by for some muffins. I forgot my tape measure in the truck. Going to help her hang some new curtains."

"Maybe I should leave. You hang curtains?" Kelli shook her head.

"Come on." Beau linked his arm through hers and pulled her towards the house.

"Aunt Kelli!" Aiden came barreling at Kelli. She barely had time to free her arm from Beau's before Aiden jumped into her arms.

"You're going to knock me over." Kelli hugged him tight.

"Mom made muffins. Come on." Aiden dragged her into the kitchen.

"Well, I didn't know you had company, or I would have called first."

Jillian gave her a "whatever" look, which immediately turned into a huge grin when Beau walked in behind Kelli. "Muffins on the table. Coffee, Kel?"

198 ·Emma Leigh Reed

"OJ if you have it." Kelli was already buttering a muffin and talking with Aiden about what they could do today.

"I just want to hang out on the beach, but mom says there is never time. She has to work again today." Aiden gave his best pouty look.

"Why don't I take him to the beach while you and Beau hang whatever it is you're hanging?" Kelli asked.

"That's okay with me. He would love it and I really need to get stuff done around here." Jillian pushed a curl from Aiden's face. "I'm sorry, buddy, things have been so crazy for me lately that we haven't gotten there."

"It's okay." Aiden pushed his mom's hand away. "Got to get my swimsuit."

Kelli watched in awe at his energy as Aiden fled the room. "Wow, does he ever do anything in slow motion?"

Jillian laughed. "You sure you're up for taking him to the beach? He can be a handful."

"We'll be fine. I think I can handle it."

A Time To Heal · 199

Kelli and Aiden spent the next few hours at the beach, riding waves, searching the rocks for shells and crabs. She didn't have a moment to think of Dan until it was time to go home.

"Can we go over to those rocks before we go, Aunt Kel?" Aiden pointed to the rocks where Kelli always looked for Dan.

She closed her eyes and swallowed hard, trying to calm the anxiousness that overtook her."Sure."

They made their way over the rocks, checking tide pools and stopping along the way to look at something closer here and there. Kelli felt his presence before she saw him. Warmth spread through her when she looked up and met his ocean-blue eyes.

"Looks like fun." Dan made his way down the rocks to where Kelli and Aiden were checking out a tide pool.

"Dan, look at this." Aiden help up a starfish.

"You know you shouldn't take them out of the water." Dan moved Aiden's hand down beneath the water level.

200 ·Emma Leigh Reed

Kelli rocked back on her heels to put a little space between herself and Dan. The air sizzled around them and Kelli fought hard to not meet his gaze. "Aiden, I should get you home."

"Aww, now?"

Kelli smiled. "Yes, now. I have to be to work in a couple of hours and still need to go home and change."

"I could stay with Dan?" The hopefulness in the boy's voice melted Kelli's heart.

Dan broke in before she could answer. "Hey, I've got to be at work too. You and I can come do this another day, though."

Kelli gave a grateful look to Dan. He simply nodded. "I'll walk you to Aunt Kelli's car." Dan held out his hand to help Aiden up.

The three of them walked across the road to the bar where Kelli's vehicle had been left. "I can always drive him home, if you want," Dan voiced.

"I've got it. He's my responsibility today, but thanks." Kelli helped Aiden into the back seat and walked around to the driver's side.

"See you tonight." Dan waved as he headed towards his vehicle.

Kelli slipped into the car. Aiden chatted all the way back to their house and was out of the car as soon as it was shut off. Kelli followed him inside at a slower pace. Jillian was curled up in her recliner with a book in her lap, forgotten now as she was listening to Aiden go on and on about all the cool things he had found at the beach.

"Thanks." Jillian gave Kelli a grateful smile. "It was nice to have a little time to myself today."

Dan sat at his kitchen table, head in his hands. On the table in front of him were all the alcohol bottles he had in the house—three bottles of vodka and two six-packs of beer. He stared at them, fighting the battle within. He wanted to reach out and just take a swig out of the vodka bottle, knowing that the warmth would spread through him and he would become numb to the pain that he felt.

Pain that he couldn't be the man that Kelli deserved, no matter how much he wanted to be that man. Pain in finally letting go of the anger at Mia and the way their marriage had ended. He desired to be a better man and Kelli brought that desire out in him. It was more than sexual tension between them. It was a desire to be better, not drink, and take chances. The desire to open his heart once again and allow someone in…someone that might, just might, be able to love him like he wanted.

He reached for the first vodka bottle. He played with the cap while he held it. Closing his eyes, he rested the bottle against his face. *No, I do not need this in my life.*

Dan stood and grabbed all the vodka. He crossed the kitchen in just a few steps to the sink and started emptying the contents down the drain. He threw the empty bottles in the trash. Hands shaking, he reached for the beer and continued the process of emptying all the alcohol down the drain. With a sigh, he sank to the floor.

I can do this…for myself. I want a better future…with Kelli.

Chapter Twenty-Three

He sat in his car across the street from The Salty Claw. The police had been too prominent the past few nights for him to cause any trouble. He was irritated even more and his temper completely out of control. He tried to rope it in so he could think more clearly. He swallowed a couple of aspirin and chased it with a swig of beer. Tonight was going to be the night, regardless of if police were around. He didn't know exactly how he was

204 ·Emma Leigh Reed

going to shut this place down, but she *would* be coming home with him. Enough was enough.

He started his vehicle and drove back to the hotel. He needed to figure out where to go from here. The vandalism didn't shut them down even for a day. How deep did the pockets of the owner go? Usually not that deep when starting a business. He had researched Beau and as far as he could tell there was no extra money there at all. He had to have a backer that wasn't listed as an owner.

Another busy night finished. Kelli had come to love the closing and the chance to relax with her friends-- family really. Beau and Jillian were more her family. Kelli helped herself to a glass of wine and stood across from Jillian. "Hear anything from Sam?"

"No. I left my cell phone there. I had cleaned out all my contacts, everything."

"Good idea." Kelli was thoughtful. "We should get you another one though, especially since you

A Time To Heal · 205

haven't gotten a phone hooked up at your house yet."

"I had thought of it, but wanted to make some more money first. I'm going to get one of those pay-as-you-go ones." Jillian finished her wine and set the glass down. "Please don't worry about me."

Kelli absently nodded. "You know I'll always worry about you and Aiden."

"Yes. But you have done so much already for us." Jillian grabbed her glass to take to the kitchen. "I've got this."

Kelli handed her now empty glass to Jillian. "I know you do, but that's not going to change my anxiety when it comes to Sam and you."

"Noted."

Jillian and Dan returned to the bar from the kitchen together. Jillian had her arm looped through his and was laughing at something he said. Kelli felt a twang of jealousy tear through her at seeing them so easily interact. Why couldn't Dan laugh with her like that? He clearly was attracted to her, yet avoided her at all costs.

Beau came out from the office. "Everybody set to leave?"

The chorus of "yes" carried them to the door. Beau locked up as everyone started to disperse. Kelli glanced back as she walked to the corner of the building. Dan was watching her as he said goodbye to Beau and Jillian. She let loose the clip that was holding her hair up and shook it down as she rounded the corner to the stairs.

Kelli slipped into a tank top and shorts. It had been a long night, yet she was wide awake. A soft knock at the door made her glance at the clock, 2:00. She glanced out the side window to see Dan with his back to the apartment. She pulled open the door.

"Hey."

Dan turned to face her. "Hey, yourself."

"What's up?" Kelli gestured for him to enter.

Kelli shut the door softly behind him and leaned against it, waiting. Dan faced her, their eyes meeting. He took one step, closing the gap between them. He boxed her in with his hands against the door on either side of her. "I needed to see you."

"Seems to me you have been doing a good job of avoiding me." Kelli stated, forcing her hands to stay at her side.

"Yes. I have avoided you. You drive me crazy with want." Dan leaned closer. Kelli could feel the warmth of his breath on her cheek. "You make me want to feel alive again." He kissed her neck softly.

"Dan…"

He pulled back and met her eyes. "Tell me you want this, too."

She closed her eyes and willed her arms to stay at her side. Kelli bit her bottom lip and opened her eyes. Dan's blue eyes searched hers. She raised her hands to rest on his waist and pulled him closer. "Yes, I want this." She pulled his shirt free from his jeans and lifted it over his head. Throwing it to the side, she ran her hands over his rock hard abs.

Dan grabbed her hands and lifted them above her head, pinning her to the door. His face was close to hers but not touching. His tongue ran over her bottom lip and she longed for him to kiss her. Kelli leaned her head forward to capture his lips, but he pulled back. "Don't rush. I think you need to learn patience."

She leaned her head against the door and closed her eyes. Torture, yet this was his idea of teaching patience. He whispered in her ear, "Keep those eyes closed."

She sighed and forced her eyes to stay shut. Dan kissed down her jaw, down her neck. She tilted her head to give him better access to that sweet spot between her neck and shoulder. He chuckled as he moved past the spot he knew she wanted him to be. Letting go of her hands, he ran his down her cheeks and neck, with his fingers dancing over her skin. Kelli pushed against the door, hands still overhead.

Dan ran his fingers over her taunt nipples as they pushed against her tank top. She moaned softly. Lifting the hem of her shirt, Dan pulled it slowly up and stopped just above her breasts. She felt his eyes on her, her eyes still closed, lips parted. Kissing her softly on the lips, suckling the bottom

A Time To Heal · 209

lip into his mouth, he gently teased her nipples, rolling them between his fingers. Kelli whimpered softly and arched her back, wanting more.

Dan broke off the kiss and moved to the base of her neck, licking her lightly. He yanked the tank top over her head and tossed it out of the way. He held the weight of her breasts in his hands, thumbs moving in circles over her nipples. She inhaled sharply as he took one nipple into his mouth and suckled her. Her hands made their way to his head, fingers entwining in his hair, pulling him closer.

Dan pulled back and picked her up. "Bedroom?"

"Down the hall." Kelli wrapped her arms around his neck and kissed him as he stumbled down the hall to the bedroom. Dan placed her on the bed and slid her bottoms off. Kelli reached for his jeans, making quick work of the button and zipper. Pulling them down off his hips, she reached for him. He closed his eyes as her hand wrapped around the length of him. He trembled and pulled back from her. Stepping out of his jeans, he pulled a condom from his back pocket.

Dan pushed her back onto the bed. His hand slid up her thigh, finding her wet warmth. He stroked her, her eyes clouding as she went over the edge. He gently kissed her, trying to slow his breathing. "I can't wait, Kel." He sat up and rolled the protection on. Nestled between her legs, he kissed her as he slid into her heat. They moved together as one, a perfect melody played together. She clung to him as she hit her peak and called out his name. Dan shuddered and kissed her deeply as he rode the crest with her.

Dan took slow breaths to steady his breathing. He settled onto his back and pulled the sheet up over them. Kelli nestled into the crook of his arm, head on his chest. He kissed her forehead and pulled her closer as she sighed.

"The A/C didn't get put on," she whispered.

"I'll get it. The one in the living room?" Dan slid out from under Kelli's arm and leg.

A Time To Heal · 211

"Mm hmmm." Kelli had her eyes closed and settled into the warmth of the bed.

In the living room, Dan reached for the power button when light caught his eye. He leaned towards the window and saw the brake lights of a sedan.

"Kelli, bring me my pants."

Kelli handed him his pants. "What's going on? You're leaving?"

"Someone's in the parking lot. Call the police." Dan slipped into his jeans and zipped them. "Make the call." He slipped his bare feet into his sneakers.

Dan crept down the stairs to the corner of the bar. He held back as he heard a door slam. Peeking around the corner, he saw a tall man walk towards the front door. He held something in his hand and flung it through the window and turned to get in his car. Dan looked at the car—black sedan. The car took off and Dan went to the front door. There was smoke filling the dining room. He unlocked the door. Smoke billowed around him. Small flames licked at the floor.

212 ·Emma Leigh Reed

He ran in and grabbed the fire extinguisher from next to the hostess station. The smoke filled the room as he sprayed the flames. Emergency lights flashed as the police cruiser came to a screeching halt in the parking lot. Dan met Phil at the doorway.

"It was a black sedan. Couldn't get a good look at the license plate."

"What happened?"

Dan placed the fire extinguisher on the floor. "Guy threw in the bottle, obviously some sort of a small bomb. Didn't start a huge fire, lots of smoke."

Kelli came around the corner, holding the phone to her ear. "Phil's here now. See you in a few." She handed Dan his shirt. "You okay?"

"Yeah. This was deliberate, though, and I want to know who did it." Agitation laced his words. "If you had been alone and asleep, this place could have gone up in smoke and you could have been hurt."

"But I'm not." Kelli grabbed his arm. "We're fine."

A Time To Heal · 213

Beau showed up, and Kelli filled him in. The fire department had arrived and the fire marshal roped off the area with the broken window. There was no doubt it was arson. Unfortunately, The Salty Claw would be shut down for the next few days until the investigation was complete and clean up could be done.

"What are we going to do?" Kelli was furious. "Who did this?"

Beau pulled her off to the side, away from the chaos. "I don't know. I don't have anyone that would want to hurt this place or me. Aaron? Where is he?"

"I don't think it would be him." Kelli rubbed her arms. "I can call him, but really, do you think it is him?"

"I don't know, Kel." Beau pulled her close. "You're chilled. Why don't you go back to your apartment?"

Kelli tensed. "I'm not being dismissed. This is my business, too, and I'm not going to just be shooed away."

"Hey, I didn't mean it like that. Stay. I don't care. I thought you were cold." Beau held up his hands in surrender. "So how did Dan get here so quickly?"

Kelli glared at him. "Don't you have someone you should be talking to? Phil?"

Beau's laughter stroked the irritation already building in her. She didn't want anyone knowing her business, especially since she didn't know how Dan would be reacting. He was prepared to stay the night and hold her, but now...with all this, who knew how his mind would go.

By the time the fire department and Phil had wrapped things up enough to leave, dawn was breaking. Kelli headed to the apartment thinking her magic brew was exactly what she needed after a sleepless night. As she entered, the living room was stifling and she realized Dan had never put the air conditioner on. She flipped the switch and sank onto the couch. She wanted coffee, but was just going to close her eyes for just a moment.

Chapter Twenty-Four

Dan poured himself another cup of coffee and one for Beau. Beau had insisted on going back to Dan's place after everyone left the fire. Dan wanted nothing more than to go to Kelli and make sure she understood he wasn't going to avoid her again. But he didn't want to say anything to Beau without talking to Kelli first.

"You're pretty quiet." Beau's voice broke through Dan's thoughts.

216 ·Emma Leigh Reed

"Just tired, as I'm sure you are." He slid the coffee mug in front of Beau and sat down.

"Yeah. Certainly no one got any sleep last night, huh?"

Dan took a sip. "You were still up, huh? Did you make it home or were you still at Jillian's?" Dan smirked at him.

"Funny. Are we going to trade interrogations here?"

Dan shook his head. "Not a chance."

They drank their coffee in silence, each engrossed in their own thoughts. Dan was the first to break the silence.

"So who do you think is behind this?"

Beau was thoughtful. "I wonder about Aaron, Kelli's ex, but I'm not sure he would really do it. I don't know. Jillian's boyfriend was abusive and she ran in the night from him, but as far as Kelli knows, he doesn't know where she is."

"Okay. So we're looking at one of two pissed off exes. Wonderful. There is nothing worse than a disgruntled, unreasonable ex."

A Time To Heal · 217

"Agreed." Beau sat back. "Kelli thinks Aaron has gone back to New England. I don't know, though. He left pretty calmly after begging her to come back. He just took the rejection all in stride."

"Meaning?"

"He never struck me as the type to not get his own way and be okay with it. She walked on eggshells for years with that guy just to keep the peace so he wouldn't show his temper."

"Does Phil have this information?" Dan drained his coffee and pointed to Beau's empty cup. "Another?"

"Sure. And yes, Phil has the information. I don't know if Kelli gave him Aaron's contact info or not."

"Well, we have a few days off. How soon before we can get in to clean?"

"Not sure. Waiting to hear back from the fire marshal, hopefully later today he will have some information."

Dan refilled coffee cups and sat back down. "So what now?"

"Take a few days and do whatever you want."
Beau drank his coffee. "I'm going to see if Jillian
wants some company. Maybe we can take Aiden to
see a few tourist attractions."

Dan laughed. "Ah ha. You've been bitten."

"You and me both, my friend. I see the way
you look at Kelli when she isn't looking. What's the
deal with treating her like she has the plague?"

Dan shook his head. "I didn't think I was ready,
but maybe that has changed. I need to talk to her."

Beau stood. "I'm going to head for home and
get a little bit of shut eye." He slapped Dan on the
back. "Don't wait too long, you might miss your
chance."

Dan nodded and finished his coffee as Beau let
himself out. He hadn't waited too long, but after last
night, after the fire, he had just left and he could
only imagine what would be going through Kelli's
mind. He picked up the phone and dialed her
number. Immediate voice mail. Either she was tired
and shut her phone off or she was avoiding him.

A Time To Heal · 219

Washing the dishes, Dan ran last night over and over in his mind. He wanted to go to Kelli and just hold her as they rested from the events of the night before. But fear struck him and he was paralyzed with it. He dried his hands and went down the hall to his bedroom. He stretched across the top of his bed and drifted off to a fitful sleep, filled with dreams of Kelli beackoning to him and Mia taunting him.

Kelli fell into a restless sleep on the couch. She avoided the bedroom. She didn't think she could bear the memories of last night. She had allowed him into her heart and it was only a matter of time before she gave up denying that she had fallen in love with him. She tossed and turned, dreams from Aaron and their final conversation to Dan walking away from her haunted her. Rejected once again.

Kelli woke in a cold sweat. Kicking off the blanket, she made her way to the kitchenette to start the coffee. She had been asleep for a couple of hours and yet felt like she hadn't slept at all. A dull ache behind her eyes indicated the start of a migraine if she didn't get some sleep. She searched for her migraine medication. It had been so long since she had to take one that she didn't remember where she had put them. Giving up on finding her medication, Kelli leaned against the counter.

Inhaling deeply, she took in the rich aroma of the coffee. Hopefully the coffee would help the headache before it flared to uncontrollable. Sex always controlled them before. She sighed. Who knew when that would happen again?

She opened her laptop and perused her emails. Noting her classes were open online, she went through syllabuses and ordered the books she would need for the coming classes. She did as much as she could to prepare for the upcoming term before closing her laptop. She wasn't used to having free time like this. A run was what she needed to clear her head.

She changed into her running shorts and a tank top. Stepping onto the beach, she stretched before starting a slow jog. She turned in the opposite direction of her usual route. A change of scenery was needed. She ran hard, pushing her usual paces. Could she outrun her thoughts? As hard as she tried, Dan invaded every crevice of her mind.

Kelli finished her run and made her way to the rocks. She sank onto the flat rock and leaned back. With her eyes closed, she allowed the sound of the waves crashing on the rocks to mentally wash over her and clear the remaining haze. Her headache dissipated with the coffee and sea air. She once again contemplated how she could have lived anywhere else her whole life but right here on the ocean. This is where she felt herself, relaxed and calm, most of the time. More than once this morning she had wondered how much worse the fire would have been if Dan had not been at her place. The thought of it brought a smile to her face despite the damages to the bar…Dan. Warmth spread through her at the very thought of him. She would wait on him for the next move. Would he go back to avoiding her or had he finally faced his demons and was able to move on? Was she a part of that moving on or had it been a one night thing?

She was amazed at how intensely and desperately she wanted it to be more. Kelli could never allow him to know that. It would only scare him off. She sighed and stood to head home. A hot shower was what she needed before she could figure how to proceed with the rest of her day.

Chapter Twenty-Five

He sat in his hotel room, kicked back on the bed. He turned in his rental car for a different one just to cover his tracks. The fire would have caused a bit of damage and he longed to ride by to check it out. Reality was he needed to stay put for the day. He was just waiting for a text or a call from her to come crawling back. He would take her back, but she would pay for thinking she could shut him out of her life.

He flipped on the TV to the local news. They had a brief mention of the fire at the new bar, The Salty Claw, yet from the pictures it looked hardly damaged at all. He sat up straight and turned up the volume. How could that be? The fire should have spread quickly. No cars had gone by while he was there; there had been no one about. He made sure of it. He cursed out loud and threw the remote across the room. He started pacing, feeling the walls close in around him.

He craved a drink and as time passed, the craving increased and only fueled his agitation. He wanted to just go grab her now and tell her she had no choice but to come home with him. *Enough of this nonsense.* He wanted his life back and he wasn't about to wait any longer for her to change her mind. He tried to end her job and obviously that wasn't going to work. He would have to make her see his way, by force if necessary.

A Time To Heal · 225

Dan paced his kitchen. No sleep, and thoughts filled with Kelli were driving him insane. He wanted to go to her and tell her they were fine, but he didn't know what to expect. Maybe she didn't want to see him. Because of all the excitement he didn't know what her reaction would have even been this morning had he been there. He turned and headed out the door. He stopped short when he saw Aiden sitting on the front porch.

"Hey, ah, Aiden." Dan crossed the lawn between the two houses and settled onto the bottom step.

"Hey." Aiden's dejected look spoke volumes for this usually energetic, happy child.

"What's the matter, bud?"

"Nuttin.' Mom, said we can't do anything cuz she doesn't know when she'll be back at work." Aiden placed his chin in his hands.

The kid knew how to milk it, that was for sure. "What did you want to do?"

"Get ice cream."

226 ·Emma Leigh Reed

Dan smiled. How he wished, someday when he had a son or daughter, that they were just like this kid. Aiden had already wormed his way into Dan's heart. "Well, go get your mom."

"Why?" Aiden sat up straight.

"Just because. Go ahead."

Aiden jumped up and ran inside. "Mom!"

Jillian came to the door, pulled by Aiden. "Hi, Dan. What's up?"

"Well, it's a gorgeous day and I think the three of us need to go get ice cream."

Jillian shook her head. "Not today."

"Yup, my treat. Come on, Jill, you can't say no to ice cream."

Jillian pointed to Aiden. "You set this up."

"No. My idea, really." Dan broke in. "Come on, after last night, we all could use a little cheering up."

"Please, Mom?" Aiden turned those adorable puppy eyes on his mom and she was lost. Dan saw the instant she caved.

"Fine."

"Good. Let's walk."

Dan and Jillian fell into a comfortable silence and Aiden talked up a storm about what he wanted to do this summer and how he couldn't wait to start school. He wanted to play soccer. Dan smiled. "How do you keep up with him?"

"It's hard at times, but other times, it's nice to have a constant chatter so I don't have to think so much."

"He's such a great kid."

"Thanks." Jillian glanced at Dan. "He hasn't had an easy life. I stayed too long in a relationship with his dad and he was exposed to things no eight year old should ever see."

"We all make mistakes. Kids are pretty resilient."

"I hope so. I just want him happy…not to grow up scarred for life, blaming me for everything." Jillian let out a small laugh. They stood in line at the small ice cream shoppe.

"Get whatever you want, kiddo." Dan placed his hand on Aiden's shoulder ignoring the shake of

Jillian's head. He enjoyed spoiling him, and Jillian. They both deserved so much more than they had gotten so far in life. Dan paid and they turned towards the common area in town.

"I think you're doing a great job." Dan pointed out the park that had a bunch of kids playing. "Let's go over there and eat our ice cream. Maybe Aiden will get a chance to meet some of the kids."

They approached the park and Aiden slid back beside Jillian. Dan noticed his shyness for the first time. "Hey, here's a free bench."

Aiden settled into between Dan and Jillian, licking his ice cream with his eyes glued to the kids playing soccer. There were about ten of them running around, playing a pickup game. The laughter was contagious as the kids laughed at themselves and mistakes that were made. A wild kick sent the ball over to the bench.

"Hey, kick it back."

Aiden looked at Dan. "Go ahead. Kick it to them." Dan took the ice cream cone from Aiden's hand.

A Time To Heal · 229

Aiden ran and gave the ball a kick to send it back to the field. There was a chorus of "yay's" as the ball came back into play. Aiden walked back to the bench slowly and took his ice cream. His eyes never left the game. Dan finished up his cone just as Aiden said he was done and handed his to Jillian.

"Want to take a closer look at the game while Mom finishes eating?" Dan stood and waited.

"Go ahead, Aiden." Jillian nodded. "I'll be right here."

Dan and Aiden approached the game and stood on the sidelines. Dan explained different rules of the game to Aiden, who absorbed it all.

"Wanna play?" A boy approached Aiden.

"I don't know how?" Aiden took a step closer to Dan.

"I'm Matt. It's easy. Just kick the ball towards the goal. You can be on my team. Come on." Matt ran back on the field, looking back and waving for Aiden to follow.

"Go ahead. I'll stay here." Dan patted him encouragingly on the back.

Aiden ran into the game and within minutes he was kicking and laughing with the kids. He made friends fast and it was obvious he had a talent for the game. Dan smiled. As Aiden ran by, he called out, "I'm going to go sit with your mom, Aiden." Aiden waved and kept playing.

Jillian watched Aiden enjoying himself for the first time since…well, forever it seemed. "Thank you." She brushed a tear away.

"He just needs a little confidence. And making friends is the best way to do that."

"I know. I just don't remember ever seeing him so happy."

Dan slid his arm around Jillian and pulled her into a hug. "Get used to it. Life is getting better for you and that little boy."

An hour passed as they kids played and Jillian sat back, relaxed. The walk home was filled with Aiden's replays of the game and his new friends, and he immediately needed to plan a date for them to come to his house. Jillian smiled at Dan. "See what you started?"

"Yup. And now I leave you to the endless chatter while I go home to peace and quiet." Dan chuckled.

Chapter Twenty-Six

Kelli cleaned the apartment until it shone. She hated not having something particular to do and wondered when the bar would be up and running again. Her apartment couldn't get any cleaner and to have to spend more time out of work was going to kill her. At least her classes were starting next week.

A knock on the door was a welcome relief. Kelli swung up on the door, hoping it would be Dan on the other side. Beau stood there with a lop-sided grin. "Expecting someone else?"

"Not at all. Come on in."

Beau settled onto the couch as Kelli sank down on the other end, legs curled up under her. "Well, heard from the fire marshal. It was definitely arson, which we knew since Dan saw the man throw it in through the window. What was Dan doing here anyway?"

"Beau…back to the fire." Kelli brushed off the question.

Chuckling knowingly, "Yeah, okay. Well, no leads on who it was, but damage was minimal. They have what they need, so we can start clean up tomorrow."

"Well, that's good news." Kelli sighed with relief.

"We'll have lost income during a couple of busy nights."

"Every night is pretty busy, anyway. We should be okay, but I hope they find this guy soon." Kelli shuddered. "How much more can he do to the bar? And why?"

Beau shook his head. "I don't know. Have you heard from Aaron?"

"No, why?"

"The Marshal couldn't reach him. I've got to say, he's a suspect in all this."

Kelli stared at Beau. "You've got to be kidding."

"I'm sorry, Kel."

"I don't think he would do this. How could he?"

"Kel, look at his past. He never took no from you, he expected you to do exactly what he wanted. You turned him down when he wanted you back. Do you honestly think he would just go home and let it go?"

A lone tear ran down Kelli's cheek. "I had hoped."

Beau pulled her close. "We'll figure it out. But if it is him, that means he is still in the area. I don't want you staying alone."

A Time To Heal · 235

"I'm not running from him. I refuse to. He commanded my life and my movements for long enough." Kelli pushed away from Beau. "Don't ask me to leave my apartment."

"I'm worried what he might do if he came up here. You've got nowhere to go if he gets in the apartment."

"I know, but do you think I would really just let him in?"

Beau stared at her. "Kel, I just don't want to see anything happen to you."

"I know, but you need to trust me a little. If I felt I was in danger, I would let you know and I would be the first to go somewhere else. But I feel safe here."

"Okay. Hey, let's grab a pizza and head to Jillian's."

"Hmmm, was that already determined by you and Jillian?"

Beau grinned. "Jillian's idea, but Aiden wants to see his Aunt Kelli."

"Not like I'm working tonight, so let's go."

Jillian's house windows were glowing with lights when Beau and Kelli showed up. They knocked on the door with three pizzas in hand. Aiden flung open the door immediately, filling in Kelli about his day at the park, meeting friends and playing soccer. Kelli trailed after him into the kitchen with Beau bringing in the rear. She stopped short, seeing Dan sitting at the table.

"Dan brought me a soccer ball...my very own," Aiden was saying.

"That's so cool. I will be at your games cheering you on," Kelli said, trying to avoid eye contact with Dan.

Jillian pulled out paper plates and filled glasses with soda. "Let's head to the living room. Beau, grab the pizzas." Jillian corralled Aiden in front of her.

Kelli turned to the door to follow Jillian. Dan grabbed her arm and turned her to him and said, "Give me a minute."

"Dan..."

He pulled her closer and kissed her gently, tasting her lips. He broke off the kiss and smiled at her. "Yes?"

"We should go eat."

"Kel, we need to talk. I don't like the way things were left last night. I wanted to stay with you."

"I wanted you there, but we should just be thankful you got up to put the A/C on."

Dan nodded. "I want to spend some time with you, beyond the physical chemistry that is between us. I want to get to know you better."

"That would be nice. Right now, I'm starving." Kelli placed a quick kiss on his lips and left the kitchen.

He sat outside the house. He couldn't help himself. He was *this* close, but she had surrounded herself with too many people. He scowled. He needed to lure her away from everyone, but how? He hadn't done enough to close the business. It was time to go right to the source.

He started the car and drove off. He would give her another day and then it was time. He would not let her say no this time. His agitation had been a constant feeling of late and it annoyed him that he was this aggravated by the circumstances. He needed control. He would not lose it again–or her. One way or another, she was his until the end.

Chapter Twenty-Seven

Kelli helped Jillian clean up from the pizza. Kelli threw the dirty paper plates away and tied up the garbage. She stepped out the back door and placed the trash in the receptacle. A chill went through her at the sensation of being watched. Her hair on her arms stood up. She glanced around and saw no one, but quickly went back inside, locking the door behind her.

"Everything okay?" Jillian asked, hearing the lock click into place.

"Yeah." Kelli brushed it off as mild paranoia after the fire at The Salty Claw.

Laughter drifted into the kitchen from the living room where Aiden was wrestling with Beau while Dan sat back throwing out instructions every so often to help Aiden overcome the half-heartedly resistant Beau.

"Beau's really good with Aiden," Kelli commented as she put the last of the soda in the refrigerator.

"Yeah, he is. Dan, too. Aiden has been so spoiled by those two. You should have seen Dan at the park earlier with him. Got Aiden involved in a soccer game and suddenly he has friends and is talking about sleepovers." Jillian shook her head. "I have never seen him so happy."

"Just proof that getting away from Sam was the right move."

"Absolutely." Jillian paused and was thoughtful. "You don't think Sam would be looking for us, do you?"

"Maybe, but where would he go? He doesn't have any idea where you would be." Kelli hoped she sounded convincing, but even as the words came out, she wasn't sure she believed them herself.

Jillian nodded. She wanted so badly to believe it, Kelli knew she clung to any piece of hope she could. "Come on, let's join the boys."

Kelli followed Jillian into the living room and stopped short. Aiden was curled up in Dan's lap, reading a book to him. Dan helped him sound out words he was unsure of. Kelli's heart skipped a beat as she watched them. She tried to glance away when Dan raised his eyes to meet hers, but she couldn't. She wanted to melt into his arms and be safe, just like Aiden was. Dan smiled and returned his attention to Aiden, but made a quiet gesture for her to join them.

Kelli sank down to the floor next to Dan and listened intently to Aiden as he finished the book. "Did you hear me, Aunt Kelli?"

"I did. You did a great job. When did you get to be such a good reader?"

"Mom and I read every night and I can read more than before. Want to hear another?"

"Of course." Aiden scampered for his room, leaving Kelli suddenly self-conscious, sitting so close to Dan.

She started to scoot away, but Aiden was back and slid in between her and Dan, pulling Kelli closer so he was nestled between them. Kelli had a sudden longing for this—the right man, a child and such intimacy as she had never known. She swallowed hard and glanced at Dan. He was watching her with a wistful look in his eyes that was gone before she could confirm it had been there.

They spent the rest of the evening listening to Aiden read. Jillian finally took pity on them and told Aiden it was time for him to go to bed. Aiden sighed and dragged his feet to the bathroom to brush his teeth. Kelli picked up the books and followed him. She placed them back in the bookcase in Aiden's room and straightened up just as he finished brushing.

A Time To Heal · 243

"PJs, kiddo." Aiden undressed and slipped into his pajamas while Kelli cleaned up the bathroom. How could one child cause such a mess with just brushing his teeth? She smiled as she placed the cover back on the tube of toothpaste and wiped up the water on the counter.

Kelli knelt next to the bed as Aiden slipped under the covers. "Mom will be right in." She gave him a kiss. "Love you, Aiden. Don't grow up too quickly, kiddo."

"Love you, too, Aunt Kelli." Aiden snuggled under the sheet.

Kelli passed Jillian in the hall as she headed for the living room. She needed to get out of here. The presence of Dan was suffocating when all she wanted to do was curl up in his arms and let him hold her. She stood just out of sight in the hallway waiting for Jillian.

"So, what's going on with you two?" Beau's voice stilled her as he spoke to Dan.

"What do you mean?"

"Come on. I saw you looking at her while she was listening to Aiden. Are you going to tell me you aren't falling in love with her?"

There was a moment of silence and Kelli strained to hear. Dan's voice finally was heard. "I don't know what I'm feeling. Is this love? All I know is I want to be with her all the time. She's incredible."

Kelli jumped a mile when Jillian grabbed her on the shoulder and whispered, "Eavesdropping? So not like you."

Kelli swatted her hand away. "Shhh."

The girls stood quietly waiting for more conversation, but Beau and Dan had fallen silent. Kelli shrugged. "I'm going to head for home."

Jillian followed her into the living room. "You don't have to leave now."

Beau stood. "Want me to drive you?"

Kelli caught the glance Beau gave Jillian and smiled. "No. You stay and hang with Jillian."

Dan jumped up. "I'll give you a ride."

"There's no need. I can walk."

A Time To Heal · 245

Dan stared at her. "Seriously? With all that has happened, you think I'm going to let you walk back to the bar alone? Not happening. Come on, I'm driving."

Kelli scowled at Dan. She hugged Jillian and Beau goodbye. She whispered into Jillian's ear, "Behave yourself."

"Same to you," was the response.

Kelli slid into Dan's sedan and put on her seatbelt. "You know, you didn't have to drive me home. I'm perfectly fine to walk."

Dan shrugged. "I had an ulterior motive."

"Which is?"

Dan put the car in reverse and backed into the street. As he put it in Drive, he smiled. "I wanted to be alone with you."

"Ahhh…and what now?"

"Kel, I just want to spend some time with you. Is that so bad?"

"Of course not, but you do realize you are extremely difficult to read. One minute you're avoiding me, the next we're…ummm…well, you're not avoiding me and now I don't know what to expect from you."

Dan chuckled. "I'm not going to avoid you, if that was what you were expecting. I know I have been a bit of an ass, but things changed last night."

"Yeah, they did. There was a fire and we are all out of a job for the moment."

Dan pulled into The Salty Claw and shut the car off. He turned to face Kelli. "That's not what I meant."

"I know." Kelli's voice was low.

"Kel, I don't know what this is between us, but there's something there. You can't tell me that you haven't felt the connection…the pull was between us even before the sex."

"I feel it, but I'm not sure I'm ready to be in a relationship."

Dan sighed. "Who said we have to jump right into a relationship? Why do we have to label it? Why can't we just see where it goes and not fight it anymore?"

A Time To Heal · 247

"Dan, my life is messy. I've been a train wreck up until now. I'm just starting to feel like I'm getting it together."

"You are not the only one whose life is messy. God, a year ago my whole life was torn right out from under me."

Kelli nodded. "Exactly. So why rush this?"

"Who's rushing? Stop trying to put up walls and push me away."

Kelli stared at him. "Thanks for the ride."

"Kelli, let me walk you upstairs."

She shook her head. "No, not tonight. I, I need some time to think." She exited the car and with a wave, she was gone from view.

Dan hit the palm of his hand on the steering wheel. He didn't handle that very well. Damn that asshole who screwed things up last night. He should have held her all night, cooked her breakfast this morning. Instead, she was putting up walls and he didn't know how to break through them. His mind was in chaos as to what he wanted, what he was feeling, and what he should be doing. Maybe time was what both of them needed.

Chapter Twenty-Eight

He sat on the edge of the hotel bed, cell phone to ear. He listened, scowling. "You couldn't even follow simple instructions!" He stood, pacing as irritation ignited in him. "I don't want to hear an explanation of why. You had one simple job. Scare the hell out of her so she would run home."

He ran his fingers through his hair, wondering how he ended up surrounded by incompetent people. "Look, Ed, I told you to take care of things. You didn't and now I'm here picking up the mess that you left behind."

"I did what you said. There was no easier way to do it and she obviously doesn't scare easy."

He lit a cigarette and inhaled deeply. "I guess I will have to finish this my way. You're out of it now. Forget you heard from me." He ended the call and threw the cell phone on the bed. He stared out the window as he smoked.

He needed to get out of this cramped space before he went crazy. This had to end…soon.

Kelli's neck prickled again with the sensation of being watched as she ran down the beach. There were a few people out already this morning setting up before it got crowded. She nonchalantly glanced around and yet no one jumped out at her as *watching* as she ran by. She hesitated about running down the peninsula today as it was so isolated. Was she just being paranoid because of the fire at The Salty Claw? She sighed, irritated at herself for allowing her mind to run away from her about such nonsense. She squared her shoulders and headed towards the dreaded lone strip that she had been running now for a month.

As she turned down the trail, she saw other runners ahead of her. A sense of relief washed through her as she realized she wouldn't be alone. Yet she couldn't shake the sensation of someone staring at her. She ran hard, trying to outrun the paranoid thoughts and pushed herself past her windedness. She finally stopped and hauled in air, bent at the waist. She had gone down and back the trail in record time. What did she think she needed to prove? Why not just go home and allow herself the chance to say no, she wasn't going to do it? She continually pushed herself out of her comfort zone regularly now and although she liked the feeling of accomplishing something she didn't think she could do, she should be okay with not having to push herself once in a while.

She inhaled deeply and walked slowly towards home. A hot shower could clear her thoughts. Kelli had tossed and turned last night, Dan filling her mind. She had been a fool to push him away, but

252 ·Emma Leigh Reed

she wasn't sure she was ready for anything more than a physical relationship. She didn't want to give her heart away again just to have it stomped on one more time. She jogged across the street and headed for the apartment.

She slowed her pace when she saw Dan sitting at the top of the steps with two travel cups of coffee in his hands. "Hey."

"Hey yourself. I probably should have called." He stood as she came up the stairs. "But I brought coffee for you to smell."

Kelli laughed. "Gee, thanks." She took the cup, lifted the lid and inhaled deeply. The rich aroma filled her senses and tension gave way. She winked at Dan as she took a sip.

"You are insane. You realize that, right?"

"Yup, and as long as *you* realize it, we should be good." Kelli led the way into the apartment and sank into the couch. "So what's going on today?"

Dan sipped his coffee. "Beau called. We can clean today. Hopefully by tomorrow or the next day we can reopen."

"They will let us reopen if the arson is unresolved?" Kelli watched Dan play with his cup.

"Yup. Apparently, they have what they need for evidence and there is no reason to keep it closed." He looked up to meet her eyes. He hoped he could keep the desire for her from his eyes. The way she was looking at him made him feel like she could see right into his soul.

"What time are Jillian and Beau coming?" Kelli stood and finished her coffee before throwing the cup out.

"In about a half hour."

Kelli nodded. "Make yourself at home. I'm going to jump in the shower real quick."

Dan nodded. How he wanted to ask if that was an invitation, but didn't want to spook her. She had pretty much bolted last night. He needed to take this slow, slower than what his body was screaming for.

Dan flipped on the TV and aimlessly watched a game show. The thought of Kelli naked, water running over her lean body...he shifted uncomfortably on the couch. He closed his eyes and let the other night run through his memory. Her eyes closed, willingness to allow him to invoke her other senses, the soft moans she had made.

"Nothing good on?" Her voice interrupted his thoughts and he kept his eyes closed for a moment before looking at her.

"No." Dan allowed his eyes to wander down her figure, taking in the tank top that clung to her and the shorts that made her legs look like they went forever-- even for the petite thing that she was. When he finally raised his eyes back up to her face, he was met with a smirk.

"Like what you see?" Kelli crossed the few steps it took to stand in front of him.

"Yeah." Dan reached out and pulled her down to straddle him. He watched her as she settled across his lap. She placed her hands on his shoulders. She moved just slightly against him and leaned forward to kiss him.

Dan closed his eyes and allowed her to control the situation. Her tongue ran across his lips and she softly sucked his bottom lip. He placed his hands on

A Time To Heal · 255

her waist to stop her movements against him. She leaned back and watched him.

"Do you know the effect you have on me?" Dan whispered.

She smiled wickedly. "I can feel it."

"Kel, it's more than that." Dan kept his eyes locked with hers. "It's not just physical."

"What do you want, Dan?"

"I want you, all of you."

"I'm not sure I'm ready for that. Why does it have to be more than it is right now?" Kelli shifted onto the couch, off his lap and faced him.

He sighed. "I don't want to ruin anything with just sex."

She smiled. "Is having sex a bad thing?"

He grabbed her hand and laced his fingers with hers. "Not at all, in fact, it's quite great, but I want more. Are you that scared to try again?"

"Yes." The word was barely more than a whisper. "I'm petrified to go that route again."

Dan raised their hands and kissed the back of Kelli's hand. "You're not the only one scared."

256 ·Emma Leigh Reed

"Then why try to define it? We're good like this." Kelli closed her eyes. She didn't want to feel the warmth of longing when she heard he wanted more. She wanted to be able to close off her heart and just have a physical relationship and let go of all the other stuff that came with having more.

He leaned over and kissed her, a soft caress. She brought her hand up around his neck and pulled him closer. His tongue teased hers, never fully giving her what she wanted. He pulled back. "One step at a time. We'll take it slow." He pulled her from the couch. "Come on. Time to go clean so we can get back to work."

They met up with Beau and Jillian downstairs. The damage hadn't been as bad as Kelli first expected. Some of the wood flooring would need to be replaced, since they were scorched, but luckily the fire hadn't gotten enough time to really start to burn before Dan had put it out. The walls were covered with smoke and soot, and there was a small amount of water damage. Had the fire not been put out before the fire department arrived, Kelli could only imagine the amount of water damage there would have been on the wood floors. The whole place reeked of smoke.

The clean up was going to take longer than a day or two. Kelli had been on the phone getting contractors in to fix the burnt floor and professional cleaners to clear the smoky smell. All in all there had been very little that they had been able to do themselves. They knew the insurance would pay for it, but all Beau kept mentioning were dollars going out the window.

Kelli and Beau stood at the bar comparing notes. "You know it will be fine." Jillian slid onto a bar stool.

"Yeah, I know." Beau sighed. "Just so frustrating. We're losing money by not being open and now this. I've got a pretty high deductible. Whoever wanted us to be closed sure did a great job."

258 ·Emma Leigh Reed

Jillian nodded. Aiden came over and slipped his hand into Beau's. "We can go to the beach. That always makes me feel better."

Beau smiled down at him. "Yeah, me too. I think that's a great idea."

"Dan and Aunt Kelli too?" Aiden looked at Jillian.

"I'd love to," Kelli broke in.

"Absolutely. Go ahead and ask Dan." Aiden ran off before Jillian had finished her sentence.

"I'm glad you two are here." Kelli closed her folder.

"I am too. This has been good for both Aiden and I." Jillian smiled a thanks. "Although I feel like I still should be looking over my shoulder all the time to see if Sam is going to walk through those doors."

"How could he?" Kelli questioned.

A Time To Heal · 259

"I honestly don't see how he would know where I would go. I never saved any emails or texts from you. Always deleted them after I read them."

"In my gut, I feel like Aaron is behind this," Beau interrupted.

Jillian looked up at Beau. "Aaron never struck me as the violent type. This seems a bit over the top for him, but then again, I don't know him. He was used to getting what he wanted and if Kel told him no, who knows how he would react. But he wanted the divorce."

"I know, but then he wanted her back. She was pretty blunt with him about saying no. Something just doesn't feel right, like this person knows one of us."

"I'm right here, you two. And I don't think it's Aaron." Kelli walked away shaking her head.

260 ·Emma Leigh Reed

The four of them had agreed to meet at the beach. Dan was going to make lunch and bring it along for all of them.

Kelli saw Beau and Jillian had beaten her to the beach. She walked up behind them and heard Beau ask Jillian, "Hey, there's a wine auction tomorrow night. I'm going to head down there and check it out. Didn't know if you would be interested in going with me?" Beau leaned back on his elbows. "We would have to stay the night there and come back the next morning."

"Sounds like fun…but there's Aiden."

"And there's Kelli…" Beau countered.

"Yup, there's me. What am I being volunteered for now?" Kelli dumped her bag next to them.

"Beau invited me to a wine auction, but I would be gone overnight." Jillian faltered.

"Of course Aiden can stay with me. Are you kidding? We haven't had a sleepover in ages." Kelli grinned. "I can't believe you hesitated to ask. Go have fun."

"Just so you know," Beau interrupted. "I'll be asking Phil to do more drivebys after all that has been going on."

Chapter Twenty-Nine

Kelli set up the movie and called to Aiden. Beau and Jillian had left earlier for their night away at the wine auction. Kelli jumped at the chance to have Aiden overnight. They had stuffed themselves on homemade pizza and then made popcorn.

"Ready?" Kelli asked as Aiden jumped onto the couch.

"Yup. You're going to love this movie."

Kelli laughed. She wasn't sure about loving it, but it was one of Aiden's favorites. She never had

A Time To Heal · 263

been into the whole science fiction thing, but Jillian had been and Aiden had caught the fever. So Sci-Fi tonight it was. They snuggled together on the couch, popcorn in their laps, and started the movie.

"Is this going to scare me?" Kelli whispered.

"Aww, Aunt Kel...it's not scary." The disgust that she had even asked the question was evident in Aiden's voice.

By a quarter of the way into the movie, Kelli found herself enjoying the storyline. A knock on the door disturbed them.

Kelli pushed Aiden aside to get up. Swinging the door open, expecting to see Dan there, Kelli came face-to-face with Sam, Jillian's ex. She tried to close the door, but with a kick the door swung wide open and he stepped into the apartment.

"Surprised to see me?" Sam shut the door behind them and clicked the lock into place.

Kelli glanced over to Aiden, who was trying to make himself smaller on the couch. The movie played unwatched in the background. "Sam, what are you doing here?"

"I came to get what belongs to me." Sam pointed to the couch. "My son."

Kelli stepped between the couch and Sam. "That's between you and Jillian. You need to wait for her."

Sam took a step closer to Kelli. "And where is my lovely woman?"

"She's not here. Aiden and I were just having a movie night." Kelli wracked her brain on how to get out of the apartment with Aiden. She was uneasy about his demeanor and knew his temper all too well.

"Don't even think of it. You can't get out. I've been watching you a while now and I know the ins and outs of this little business adventure of yours."

"You were the one that started the fire." It was a statement rather than a question and relief went through Kelli to know that Aaron hadn't been behind it.

"I was a little disappointed at the lack of damage." Sam's eyes glinted with meanness.

A Time To Heal · 265

Aiden stood and inched his way towards the hallway.

"Where are you going, son?"

Aiden froze. "Bathroom."

"Make it fast," Sam barked.

Aiden ran down the hallway and the door slammed behind him. Kelli prayed that he would stay there. She glanced around to see where she had left her cell phone.

"Sit down." Sam pushed Kelli backwards to the couch.

"Look, what do you want?"

Sam paced the floor. "I want Jillian and my son, back home where they belong. It's your fault they left."

"My fault? Your beating Jillian up had nothing to do with it?"

"I never beat her up. I kept her in line. There's a difference."

Kelli stood up. "Keeping her in line doesn't mean breaking bones and leaving bruises."

Sam stepped in front of her. She went to take a step back and sat back down as the couch hit the back of her legs. "Stay seated, Kel. You wouldn't want me to keep you in line, too, would you?"

Kelli watched Sam resumed his pacing, his agitation evident with every step. She studied him. He had no visible weapons, but of course that didn't mean he didn't have one. Kelli also knew his hands were weapon enough. He was a former boxer and could beat the living crap out of anyone that came his way. She had seen the evidence in Jillian after one of his rages and she had seen back home the evidence in locals after bar fights he had been in. She needed to get Aiden out of here.

Kelli listened carefully to the sounds of the apartment. There had been no toilet flush, which could mean that Aiden was just hiding out in the bathroom. There was a small window in her bedroom that led to a fire escape, but she hadn't heard the sounds of footsteps on the metal. Would Aiden have thought to get out of the apartment? Was her cell phone in the bedroom and would he call for help? The poor boy was eight years old. He shouldn't have to be thinking about how to escape and save his life. The weight of the responsibility of keeping Aiden safe for Jillian was overwhelming. Kelli sat back on the couch and waited. Sam was engrossed in his pacing, obviously trying to think his way out.

"Shut that damn movie off." Anger laced Sam's words.

Kelli picked up the remote and hit off. The silence was deafening once the TV was off. Kelli waited for Sam to say something else, but the pacing continued, wearing on her nerves. She wanted nothing more than to get past him. She envisioned hitting him over the head, but nothing was close by for her to grab. He towered over her anyway and she doubted that she would have the strength to cause any damage. She certainly didn't want to enrage him anymore than he already was.

"Where is that damn kid of mine?" Sam paused suddenly in his movement and looked up the hallway.

268 ·Emma Leigh Reed

"He probably just wants to stay out of sight. As you know, there is no other way in or out of the apartment." Kelli prayed Aiden was already gone.

Sam looked down the hallway, glanced at the doorway and then to Kelli. She saw on his face the predicament he was in. He couldn't leave Kelli in the living room to go look for Aiden or she could bolt out of the apartment. Though he didn't seem to get that Kelli would never leave Aiden behind. She wasn't sure if he was still back in the bathroom, but she had to keep him safe somehow.

"Go get him." Sam gestured down the hall.

Kelli stood and moved slowly down the hall. She entered the bedroom and saw the window still half open as she had left it. She knocked on the bathroom door. "Aiden?"

No answer. "Open the door." Sam's voice startled her and she turned to see him in the doorway. Crap, she was even more boxed in than before. She tried the door, but it was locked. "Aiden, open the door. It's okay."

A Time To Heal · 269

Silence strained in the room. There was not a sound coming from the bathroom. Kelli glanced around and spied her cell phone on her nightstand.

"Get out of the way." Sam pushed her back towards the bed as he pounded on the door. "Aiden, open up. Now!"

Kelli grabbed the cell phone and slipped it in her pocket. She was so focused on getting the phone without being seen, she jumped when Sam kicked in the bathroom door. The door bounced off the shower tub unit and came back towards the splintered frame. Sam pushed it wide open and looked around. He looked in the tub. No Aiden.

"What the hell? Where did he go?"

Kelli trembled. "I don't know." She prayed he had made it down the fire escape, but wondered how he managed to get the screen back in place so quietly. He was eight.

Sam started searching the room. He looked under the bed, tore the closet apart, throwing clothes everywhere. "Where else could he be?"

Kelli stared at him defiantly. "It's not like the apartment is that big, look around. Do you think he could be anywhere else?"

Sam stepped towards her. "Don't push me, Kelli."

Chapter Thirty

Sam paced the living room floor. Had Ed done his job, he wouldn't be here right now. It became suddenly very clear to him that there was no way out of this once he stepped over that line and took Aiden. If caught, he would become a convicted criminal. There was no reprieve from kidnapping a child. All he wanted was for Jillian to come home. He knew he had a temper he couldn't control, but damn it, she wasn't going to run out on him.

272 ·Emma Leigh Reed

Damn, it wasn't supposed to go this way. *Think, man. Make a move and get the hell out of Dodge.* He continued to pace and glance down the hall where Aiden had disappeared. Nothing had gone smoothly since he first found out where Kelli had moved to. He knew the stories she was putting in Jillian's head and it just stoked his anger, taking it out more and more on Jillian.

"Where's Jillian?" Sam stopped pacing.

"She's had a night away. Some alone time."

"Really? Some alone time? Well, what a great mother she is. I'll have to nominate her for the mother of the year award." Sam smirked.

He watched Kelli shift on the couch. She was lying to him. He stepped closer to her and stopped. He had to be careful how he treated her if he wanted answers.

Kelli waited while Sam paced some more. The rage coming from him was intimidating. She didn't know how to get a text to Dan being in such close

A Time To Heal · 273

proximity. If Sam found the phone on her, she knew her life would be in danger.

Sam looked around. He stared at Kelli just sitting there watching him. "You're not as tough as I thought you would be." He sneered at her.

"What did you expect?" Kelli's mind raced with the possibilities of how this was going to end. Any scenario she played in her mind ended badly for her. The thought she kept clinging to was that she had fallen in love with Dan and maybe life was really too short to block off your heart.

"I anticipated a fight from you. After all, didn't you tell Jillian she should take kickboxing classes?"

"How did you know that?"

Sam's cruel laughter filled the apartment. "Yup, she thinks that I don't know things. She thinks if she deletes emails and text I don't know."

Kelli thought carefully about what emails she had sent to Jillian. She had given Sam her exact location if he had read the emails. Jillian thought that she got rid of them, but Sam must have been reading everything Kelli sent her.

274 ·Emma Leigh Reed

"You seem so shocked." Sam sat down on one of the stools at the kitchen counter. "Did you really think I was just so stupid that Jillian could get away with this?"

"Get away with what? She wanted out of the relationship. That's not a crime."

"She took my son from me," Sam snapped.

"You never showed an interest in Aiden. Why now?"

"She won't have him. If I can't, she won't either." The threat hung in the air between them and Kelli tried to hide her fear at the danger Aiden was in. This man was more delusional than she had ever thought.

"Come on." Sam gestured for Kelli to get up.

"Where are we going?"

Sam pushed her towards the door. "We're going to find the boy. He couldn't have gotten far."

Kelli balked. "You can't just ride around looking for him."

"I can and I will. You better pray that kid knows how to hide." He shoved her out the door

A Time To Heal · 275

and Kelli started down the stairs. There was a white sedan parked in the parking lot.

"Get in." Sam got in the driver's seat and started the car.

Kelli buckled her seat belt. "Where are you going to start?"

"At Jillian's place. The kid probably went home."

Kelli watched out the window as they drove. At least they would be close to Dan's. If she could just get away...

Sam drove slowly past Jillian's house. The lights were off and there was no sign of anyone home. Dan's house next door had a light on in the living room and Kelli wished she could reach him. Sam circled around the block and parked on the small street behind the house. Kelli could see a clear view of Jillian's back door.

"It was you."

"What was?"

"You were watching us the other night when I took out the trash."

Sam chuckled. "Yup. You seemed to be a little paranoid."

"I knew someone was watching. You have been watching me run, too."

Sam nodded. "Yeah, but you weren't who I was really after. Honestly, you have been nothing but a thorn in my side all these years."

"I'm sure. You don't like strong women who stand up for themselves. Bullies hate that."

Sam grabbed her arm in a vice like grip. "Don't be too mouthy with me, Kelli. You're only here until I find the boy." He let go of her arm.

Kelli rubbed the spot, knowing she would have a bruise there tomorrow...if she was still alive. Kelli prayed Aiden wasn't here. She mentally called to Dan, wishing they were connected enough that he would feel something was off.

"Let's go." Sam grabbed Kelli's hand and dragged her across the front seat of the car and out the driver's door.

"Where?"

"We're going to check the house. Don't even think of uttering a sound. I will knock you out right here if you do." He pulled her along behind him. She stumbled over rocks and sticks, and yet he just kept yanking her along.

They arrived at the back door and Sam tried the knob. It was locked. He pushed Kelli off to the side as he kicked in the door. The sound of splintering wood broke the silence. Kelli straightened, waiting for Dan's back light to come on. She prayed he heard it.

Sam yanked her inside and closed the broken door the best he could. He pushed her ahead of him, out of the kitchen. "Go search his room and the bitch's room. Don't turn on the lights."

Kelli went from room to room, searching with what little light came in from the street. "Why not?"

"Trying not to call attention to us. Forget it."

The house was empty. Kelli breathed a sigh of relief. She paused outside of the bathroom. "I need to go. Can I have a few seconds?"

"Do I look stupid?"

278 ·Emma Leigh Reed

Kelli turned to face him. "Look, there is no window in this bathroom. Where am I going to go?"

"Fine. Make it quick and don't lock the door."

Kelli shut herself in the bathroom and slipped her cell phone out of her pocket. She sent a quick text to Dan. *Call 911. Same has me at Jills. Aidens gone..*

She made sure her phone was on silent in case Dan texted her back and flushed the toilet. Slipped the phone back into her pocket, she opened the door and walked right into Sam.

"Let's go." Sam prodded her along to the back door where they ran across the back yard to the car. Kelli gave a quick glance to Dan's house, but saw nothing. The lights were out. She cursed under her breath in frustration.

Sam threw the car in gear and took off. He drove aimlessly around the back streets of town. "Where would he have gone?"

Kelli shook her head. "I honestly don't know. He's new to town, Sam. He probably doesn't have a clear sense of direction yet and it's dark."

"Who are his friends?"

"I don't know."

Sam pounded his fist against the steering wheel. "Don't lie to me!"

"I'm not." Kelli huddled against the door. Sam's anger was escalating and she had no idea what he would do if he was pushed over the edge.

Chapter Thirty-One

Dan read the text a second time. He dialed Phil at the Police Department and filled him in. He had just arrived in the parking lot of The Salty Claw when the text came through. Damn, she had been right next door to him and he didn't even know it. He ran up the stairs to Kelli's apartment and found the door wide open. There was nothing out of place to imply a struggle had ensued.

Dan didn't know this Sam guy, but only knew about him from things Beau had said. Here they all thought Aaron had been behind the vandalism, but Dan now wondered if Sam wasn't the culprit. He shut the door behind him and started back to his vehicle. Where would Aiden have gone? He had a momentary sense of relief that the young boy wasn't with Sam and Kelli, but then panic ensued, wondering where he was. He was too young to be wandering the streets alone.

Phil had told him he would check out Jillian's place, so Dan turned his vehicle towards home. By the time he arrived at Jillian's, there were two police cruisers in the front yard with lights flashing. Dan exited his car just as Phil came out from the back of the house.

"Nothing. They're gone." Phil shook his head.

"What now?" Dan leaned against his car.

"Well, you should call Jillian and get her back here. We are going to need her here when we find the boy."

"What about Kelli?" Dan stood. He knew Aiden was a priority, but Kelli was his top priority.

282 ·Emma Leigh Reed

"I have my men cruising the streets looking for unknown vehicles and for the boy. Trying to kill two birds with one stone."

"What can I do?"

Phil put his hand up. "You can look for the boy, but I don't want you interfering with us catching this guy."

"I don't want Kelli hurt."

"None of us do, Dan. Trust us."

Dan sighed in frustration. "Fine. But keep me posted."

Dan backed out of the driveway and turned towards the park. He had no idea where to start looking, but he knew he wasn't going to sit around and do nothing. He checked his cell phone again, but there hadn't been another text. He parked at the field in the center of town. He punched Beau's number into his cell phone. This wasn't a phone call he wanted to make.

"Hey, what's up?" Beau's voice was carefree, obviously having a good time.

Dan sighed. "Hey man. I need to tell you something that you need to pass on Jillian. It's not an easy call to make."

"What is it?" Beau's voice dropped a decibel and Dan heard a door shut. "I'm outside now. What happened?"

"Jillian's ex is in town. He surprised Kelli at her apartment. Apparently Aiden got away and no one knows where he is, but Sam has Kelli."

"Shit. We're on our way back. I'll call you from the car." The phone went silent and Dan sat there. Thank God Jillian had Beau with her, but he knew the heartache of the unknowing if your loved one was alive or not. He had to find Kelli and Aiden.

Sam was from out of town. He wondered if the police had checked hotels. Being a tourist area, Dan could only imagine that they were all full. He had no idea what Sam's last name was or what he would be driving. The car he saw the night of the fire was a black sedan. Well, it was all he had to go on. He turned towards the road known as Hotel Strip. This area was appropriately named with 45 hotels lining the road most of which were inexpensive chain hotels with an occasional locally owned hotel sitting awkwardly out of place amongst the others. It was going to be a long night. The police must have had the same thought, as there were cruisers at some of the hotels.

Dan turned toward the bar again. Would they show up there? His cell phone rang just as he turned onto the main road. "Hello?"

"Hey. We're on the road. Jillian wants to know if there's news. You're on speaker."

"I've got no news right now. Everyone is out searching for both Aiden and Kelli. Any idea, Jillian, where Aiden might go?"

"I would have thought he would have gone to you or gone home. But he doesn't know the area that well." Her voice broke as she started to cry again.

Beau broke in. "Have you checked the rocks at the beach where you and Kelli go?"

"I'll head there now." Dan turned at the next intersection. "I'll let you know what I find."

It tore at his heart to hear Jillian crying. He had to find Kel and Aiden. Instead of pulling into the parking lot at The Salty Claw, Dan drove past and parked at the beach parking lot. He exited the vehicle and sprinted to the rocky area. It was a good hideout from the world; he knew that only too well.

Dan rounded the rocks to the flattened rock where he always sat for hours. Empty. He cursed out loud. "Aiden!" He called and called until he was hoarse. He ran down the beach further, but there were no signs of anyone being there.

He trudged back to his car and sat staring at the water. Where could he be? His cell phone chimed with a text message. *White sedan, at gas station on Elm.* Dan threw the car in drive and sped out of the parking lot. With his free hand, he dialed Phil's number and conveyed the text message to him. He prayed they were closer than he was.

286 ·Emma Leigh Reed

Kelli cowered near the door as she tried to put some distance between herself and Sam. "Where are you going?" Kelli's voice broke into his thoughts.

"Not sure yet. Still looking for the kid."

"This is insane, Sam. You can't find him in the middle of the night, in the dark, with no clues as to where he went."

"You seem so sure of that. And I'd watch calling me insane…"

Frustration poured over Kelli. She was in no position to argue with him. She had nowhere to go. "You can't just drive in circles."

"I can do what I want, remember that." Sam glanced over at her.

"Why not just go back to the hotel or my apartment? Maybe Aiden came back there?" Kelli was desperate to get somewhere, hopefully where there were people.

He backhanded her. "He won't go back to your apartment. Damn it, I'm not stupid. And you saw the cops at the hotel. Shut up."

Kelli brought her hand to her face. She tasted blood on the inside of her mouth where she had bit her lip. She couldn't push him. He already was spiraling out of control.

"Want to tell me who the kid would've told to have police combing the town?"

Kelli cowered close to the door. "I don't know."

"Or was it you?"

"How could I tell someone?"

Sam pulled behind The Salty Claw. It was pitch black on the back side of the building. No one would see the car. He grabbed her arm once again and yanked her across the driver's seat. "Open the kitchen door."

Kelli keyed in the keyless lock code and entered the kitchen. She went to flip on the light and her hand was slapped down. "Don't touch it."

"You can't see in here." Kelli tried to step away from him, but Sam grabbed her arm again.

"Which means you will stay close to me and not try to sneak around in the dark." He gripped her

288 ·Emma Leigh Reed

elbow tighter. "Don't even think of trying to outsmart me. It won't end well for you."

Kelli grimaced at the pain in her arm. "Are you going to stand here at the door?"

"Walk towards the office, slowly."

Kelli thought about running him into the counter, but with the death-grip he had on her elbow, she would be the one who'd be hurt. She moved cautiously through the kitchen and into the dining room. Turning left, she moved past the bar and into the office. It was small and no light came in the window. Sam jerked her around and she collided with his chest.

He ran his free hand down the side of Kelli. "Maybe I should put you to use before I get rid of you."

Kelli trembled and tried to move away. Sam released her elbow, but snaked his arm around her waist before she could move. He pulled her against him. "What the…" He pushed her back a step and felt over her pocket. "What's in the pocket?"

"Nothing."

He reached in and pulled out her cell phone. Sam pushed her further into the room and Kelli stumbled, falling to the floor. She slid away, trying to get closer to the desk. Sam pushed a button on the phone and it lit up the room. "No outgoing calls." He glanced at her. "That's far enough. Oh, look here. You sent your boyfriend a text while we were at Jillian's."

He kicked the office door shut. "Maybe it's time I sent him one too." He quickly typed a message and pushed send. An evil laugh filled the room as he pocketed her phone.

Chapter Thirty-Two

Sam paused as lights swept past the office window. The wild goose chase had started. Who could be here? He glanced down to Kelli sitting on the floor. She was a sly one. He glanced at the door. The lights were gone. Either someone had just turned around in the restaurant parking lot or they found his car. He needed an escape route. If they went out the front, he was nowhere near his car.

"Sam…where the hell are you?" Ed's voice broke through the silence.

A Time To Heal · 291

Sam pulled open the office door. "What the hell are you doing here?"

"The police are everywhere looking for you. What the hell did you do?" Ed stepped into the office and Sam shut the door behind him. Ed held a flashlight by his leg, giving off just enough light to see.

"Were you followed?"

"No way, man. I know how to lose a tail if I had one. No one would associate me with you, anyway."

Sam ran his fingers through his hair. He could feel Kelli's eyes on him and knew he had to keep her still. "How did you know where to find me?"

Ed shrugged. "Seriously? I've been tampering with this place for weeks now."

"You?" Kelli started to stand.

"Stay put, Kelli, or you won't even step foot out of here." Sam turned towards Ed. "Shut your mouth!"

292 ·Emma Leigh Reed

"I didn't sign up for a kidnapping, man. I want out of this." Ed paced the office floor, throwing glances in Kelli's direction.

"Look, this will all be over soon. I need to find my son and get out of here."

"You won't find him here," Kelli interjected.

Sam slammed his hand against the wall. "This is your fault. Damn it, Jillian never would have left if it wasn't for you."

"Look, I'll go look for the kid. Drive around some and see what I can find. You need to find someplace to lay low." Ed started for the door.

Sam stepped in front of him. "If you even think of doublecrossing me, it won't end well for you."

"I'm not stupid, man. I know what has to be done." Sam stepped back and allowed Ed to walk through the door. Moments later lights swept through the window again as Ed sped away from the restaurant.

"You put him up to all the damage around here?" Kelli pushed back against the desk.

A Time To Heal · 293

"If the business closed, I figured you'd come back before Jillian took off then she would stay put. But, damn it, you wouldn't just leave things alone."

"Do you hear yourself? You are out of control, Sam." Kelli suddenly was quiet.

"Want to voice anymore stupid remarks?" Sam sneered at her. "Just shut up and let me think."

He paced the room in front of the door. He had more of an issue now that Ed had blabbed about doing the damage to the restaurant. If he let Kelli go, he would be caught in no time. The room was closing in on him, and panic closed his chest. He took a gulp of breath and tried to quiet the anxiety rising up in him.

Chapter Thirty-Three

Dan arrived at the gas station, not at all surprised to see police cruisers, yet no sign of Kelli. Phil wandered over to his car. Dan put down the window.

"I spoke with the clerk. There hasn't been a white sedan here all night."

Dan handed over his phone to Phil, the text message clearly on the screen. "Why then?"

Phil handed it back to him. "I'm assuming he found the cell phone on Kelli. He probably sent it to throw us off."

Dan dropped the phone into his cup holder. "What now?"

"We keep looking."

Dan shook his head. "This is going nowhere."

"I know you feel that way, but it takes time." Phil glanced at a couple of his patrolmen finishing up. "Look, meet me at Kelli's apartment. I want to look around there and maybe we can get a feel for at least which way Aiden went."

Dan nodded. He called Beau on the way to Kelli's and gave the latest, albeit nothing to really report. Beau had guessed they were still a couple of hours away, and that was while pushing it way beyond the speed limit.

Dan drove to The Salty Claw knowing Phil was right behind him. They drove into the parking lot and all was dark. As they exited, Dan pointed to the stairs on the side of the building. Phil went first up the stairs and entered the apartment. Dan pointed out how nothing was out of place.

"Did you check the bedroom?"

Dan shook his head, and led the way down the hall. They looked around at the clothes on the floor. "He was searching in here, but for what?"

Dan checked the bathroom and saw the broken door. Phil was checking the window. "There's a fire escape out here." He shined his flashlight down the stairs and around the area below. His light glanced off something and he turned the beam to see what it was. "Well, what do you know?"

"What?" Dan was at his side in a second.

"Looks like a white sedan."

Dan turned and started for the front of the apartment. "They must be in the bar."

"Wait a minute." Dan stopped and faced Phil.

"We don't have a minute."

Phil held up his hand. "Yes, we do. I'm calling for back up and you're not going in with me. We don't know if this guy is armed or not."

A Time To Heal · 297

Dan started to protest, but knew it was futile. "Fine. But I'm not leaving."

"You just stay out of the way and let us do our jobs."

Dan paced in the parking lot while Phil instructed his men on what needed to be done. He nodded when Phil sent him a raised eyebrow, knowing full well that Phil meant business about Dan staying out of the way. Fear gripped his stomach and he struggled to keep himself in control. If anything happened to Kelli, he would never forgive himself. He couldn't lose her now—he just couldn't. He hadn't even realized how much the crack in his heart had widened to allow her to enter in.

Kelli sat on the cool floor, leaning against the desk. Her eyes had adjusted to the darkness and she could make out Sam pacing in front of the door. "What are you going to do now?"

Sam stopped and glanced her way. "Just be quiet."

Kelli wanted to needle him, but he was still on edge and she was running out of energy. Her chest hurt from anxiety, wondering where Aiden was. Had Dan gotten her texts? If he had, did he go on a wild goose chase with Sam's text from her phone? She felt one of her migraines starting in the back of her eye and she willed it not to become full blown.

She had no idea how long they had actually been in the bar, or really how much time had passed since Sam had shown up at the apartment. Kelli could only imagine the frantic heartache that Jillian was enduring if she knew that her son was missing at this point. Kelli clung to the hope that Aiden wasn't actually missing, but that he had found someone to help him.

Kelli squared her shoulders. She couldn't just sit here and do nothing. She inched to the side, keeping her back against the desk. She just needed to get around behind it. Sam wouldn't be able to see her and if she could get him to circle the desk she could run for the door. She moved another inch and waited. She had to strain to really make him out and knew he couldn't see her well, either. Beau had kept the blinds down in the office to keep it from heating up so with the sun shining in. That worked in her favor right now. The disadvantage would come when she made it to the other side and her not being able to really see him, either.

It had to work. "Kelli, get up."

She looked up and saw Sam standing against the door. "I'm tired. Can't I just sit a while longer?"

"Get up!" He started for her and she knew she was running out of time. She pushed herself off the floor. She moved quickly to the other side of the desk and waited. His shadowy figure came toward her and she moved to the edge of the corner.

Sam started around the desk to reach her and she bolted for the door. She knocked over the chair as she ran by and heard Sam crash into it. She opened the door just as Sam grabbed her and yanked her back. Suddenly they were in the direct light of a flashlight. Sam put his hand up to shield his eyes, letting go of his grip on Kelli, who moved towards the light.

300 ·Emma Leigh Reed

Phil grabbed Kelli and pulled her into the dining room. Two other officers proceeded to apprehend Sam. Kelli closed her eyes and sank into a chair that Phil held out for her. "Any word on Aiden?"

"No, unfortunately, not yet." Kelli glanced up at him.

"Kelli!" Dan's voice broke through her haze of her migraine. She stood and in a moment was pulled into his embrace. "Thank God you're fine."

"We've got to find Aiden." Kelli's voice caught as she tried to hold back the sobs.

"I know. I know." Dan kissed her gently. "We'll find him."

"Does Jillian know what happened?"

Dan sighed. "Yes.She and Beau are on their way back. They should be here in about an hour."

"I let her down." Tears started flowing down Kelli's cheeks. "How can she ever trust me again?"

"You didn't let her down. You didn't have a choice. Aiden was smart and got out of there."

"But we don't know where he is." The sobs overtook her as she leaned against Dan's chest. He held her close and let her release the anxiety that had been pent up for the past few hours.

Phil walked over and laid a hand on Kelli's shoulder. "We are going to need a statement from you, but it's okay for you to stop by tomorrow by the station and we'll do it then."

Kelli nodded.

"We're still looking for him." Phil nodded to Dan and walked off.

Kelli looked around the bar. This was supposed to be her safe place, her chance to start over and here everything was a mess once again. She turned toward Dan, tears welling up in her eyes.

He pulled her close. "It's okay."

"It's never going to be the same, is it?" Kelli pulled away and walked towards the kitchen. Dan was just a step behind her.

"Kel, it will be." He grabbed her hand and she jumped and pulled back. "Hey…"

302 ·Emma Leigh Reed

"Sorry. My arm is so sore from Sam pulling on it. That's all." She absently rubbed her elbow.

They made their way outside to Dan's car. Phil was standing there with a map of the town. Sam had already been taken to the station. "Good, there you two are." Phil stretched the map over the hood of his car. He pointed out different areas his men were checking for Aiden. "Kelli, any idea where else we could be looking?"

Kelli shook her head. "I don't know. The rocks, maybe?"

"I checked. He wasn't there." Dan answered, then glanced at Kelli. "Where else has he gone with you?"

Kelli closed her eyes. Her head was killing her. "I don't know. I'll be right back." She started for her apartment and heard Dan calling after her. "Give me one second."

She ran up the stairs and entered the apartment. She hesitated for a brief moment. Would she feel at ease here again? She quickened her pace to the kitchenette and reached overhead to the cabinet over the fridge for her migraine medication. She didn't have the luxury of going to bed right now and sleeping this off.

Kelli grabbed two bottles of water and headed back outside. Opening one of them, she took a swig and washed down the medication. Dan and Phil's heads were bent together over the map, strategizing where they should go. She handed the other bottle of water to Dan and took a deep breath.

"My cell phone…Sam took it."

Phil nodded. "We'll get it back for you."

Dan stepped away from them as he answered his phone. "Kel's right here." He turned and handed the phone to Kelli. "Jillian."

"I'm so sorry." Tears started flowing once again.

"Don't be sorry, hon, as long as you are okay. We'll find Aiden."

"I should have protected him." Kelli reached for Dan's hand.

"I taught him how to get out of the house if Sam was out of control. He was doing what he knew to do. Beau and I will be there in thirty minutes. We'll call you when we're there."

"Okay." Kelli handed the phone back to Dan, who talked briefly.

Phil explained how they were going to start going door-to-door. Kelli nodded. "I don't know where else to look."

"Think, Kel. Where would he have gone with you or with his mom?"

"Dan took him to the park with Jillian. He met some friends while playing soccer. He has walked with me along the beach, sat at the rocky area, walked down the peninsula."

Phil continued to look at the map. "Okay. Here's a couple of flashlights. Start walking the beach, sweep the area in the water also and just look in all areas of the rocks." He turned to Dan. "Call and check in every fifteen minutes."

Chapter Thirty-Four

They had been walking for what seemed like hours. There had been no talking other than an occasional, "See anything?" They had gone slowly, searching all the rocky areas and sweeping their lights over the water.

Kelli sank down onto the flat rock in the rocky cove. "We're never going to find him."

Dan sat down next to her and wrapped his arm around her. "We will. Have faith."

Kelli laughed. "Faith is something I don't have."

"Well, maybe it's time to change. Look at how things have worked out. Sam has been caught, you were really uninjured except for some bruising. Things could have been a lot worse."

Kelli laid her head on Dan's shoulder. "I know. I just wanted to move here to have a fresh start, and instead I have dealt with my ex, now Jillian's ex, lost Aiden…"

Dan kissed her forehead. "Made me fall in love with you."

Kelli looked up at him. Her shoulders stiffened and she shook her head briefly. "We should keep moving."

Dan sighed. Now was not the time to push this issue. She needed to hear that he had fallen in love with her and Dan couldn't be more thrilled to realize that he had learned to love again. They started down the beach further, headed towards the running trail on the peninsula.

"How would he have gone down this far?"

A Time To Heal · 307

Dan shook his head. "I don't know. Disoriented in the dark, maybe?"

They continued on in silence, each lost in their own thoughts. Kelli kept running the thought that Dan loved her through her mind. He really did. She concentrated on the past few weeks and what her feelings were. She missed him when they didn't connect during work. Kelli had been miserable when he had been avoiding her. Sex had been great between them and she wanted more of that, but was that love? Did she dare open her heart and be vulnerable to yet another man?

Dan stopped at the trail entrance. "This area is so remote. Do you really think he would come down here?"

"I don't know. But we need to check." Kelli laced her fingers with Dan's. "I need to find him before Jillian gets back."

Dan kissed her softly. "We'll find him. If not here, we'll keep looking." They continued down the trail, swinging their flashlights from side-to-side looking for anything out of the ordinary and calling the boy's name. The trail was a mile long to the end of the peninsula and seemed to take forever to walk. Kelli was used to running the mile in six minutes. She was itching to run to the end and prove to herself that Aiden wouldn't be there.

"Searching takes time. We can go faster on the way back, but slow down." Dan talked softly to her. Kelli felt like she was going to explode when they came to the end of the trail. The end of it was marked by benches along the rocky shore. Kelli had sat here numerous times to catch her breath. She swung her light back and forth. The last bench held a bunched up sweatshirt, or so it seemed.

"What's that?" Kelli pointed to the bench.

Dan walked down and slowly approached it as it started to move. "Aiden?" Dan ran around to the front side of the bench and gathered the small boy in his arms. His face was tear-stained and he was shivering. Kelli wrapped her arms around both Dan and Aiden, kissing Aiden's head.

"Aunt Kelli, Dan."

A Time To Heal · 309

"We're here. Are you okay?" Kelli ran her hands over his arms and legs.

"I'm okay. I got lost going to Dan's. I got away from Daddy, though."

Kelli laughed and kissed his forehead. "Yes, you did. You were so brave."

Dan picked him up to carry him. "Come on. Let's go find Mom."

They started down the trail and Kelli, using Dan's phone, placed a call to Jillian. "We've got him and he's fine."

"Oh, thank God. We're just coming into town. We'll meet you at your place." Kelli hung up and smiled at Dan. A good outcome all around. And now Jillian and Aiden were truly safe from Sam. She dial and notified Phil that they had found Aiden.

They arrived back at The Salty Claw and Beau and Jillian were waiting out front. Jillian was pacing in front of the building and as soon as she spied them, she sprinted to Aiden. Grabbing him from

Dan, she held him close. "Oh, buddy, you did so good."

"I remembered what you taught me." Aiden laid his head on Jillian's shoulder. "Can I go to bed now?"

Jillian smiled and held on to him tightly. "Yes, we'll go home."

Dan had pulled Beau aside and explained about the back door at Jillian's. "We need to fix that tonight before she spends the night there."

Beau nodded. He glanced up as Jillian and Kelli approached. "Why don't you guys spend the night with Kel tonight? It might do you all some good to be together."

Jillian pondered the thought. Kelli placed a hand on Jillian's back. "I could use the company, that's for sure. You and Aiden can have the bed. I'll sleep on the couch."

Beau and Dan walked the girls to the apartment. Beau went with Jillian to the bedroom to get Aiden into bed. Dan pulled Kelli close and claimed her lips. It was a gentle, yet demanding kiss. Kelli leaned into him, sighing softly as she tilted her head to allow him better access. A soft throat clearing brought the kiss to an end.

"Don't mean to interrupt, but we probably should get to Jillian's and get that door fixed." Beau spoke behind them.

Kelli searched Dan's face. "I'll see you tomorrow, count on it." Dan said as he gave her another quick kiss.

Chapter Thirty-Five

A week had passed since that frightful night. Kelli's nightmares were starting to lessen. Aiden seemed no worse for wear from the whole ordeal. Despite all that had happened, The Salty Claw had gotten cleaned up and had reopened for business.

Music was playing and Kelli was tapping her foot in time to the bass as she manned the hostess station. They were full once again and patrons seemed happy to have them back. Jillian and Deb had been outright running with drinks and food.

A Time To Heal · 313

Kelli managed to avoid Dan, with the exception of when Beau and Jillian were around. They hadn't had any time to have a real conversation, and Kelli knew she was running out of time. She had been searching her heart and mind for what she was feeling, and then fighting those feelings constantly. Dan had been patient, but tonight before work had insisted that afterwards they were taking a walk to the rocky cove to talk. It was now midnight and she had two hours to get her thoughts together. Kelli finally knew what she wanted, but was unsure how Dan would react when she worked up the courage to tell him.

Time certainly wasn't standing still tonight. The clock was ticking and with each passing second, Kelli became more and more certain of what she needed to do. By the time the clock struck two and Kelli had locked the doors, she was feeling more relaxed than she had all week. Making a decision had a positive affect like that.

Kelli was chatting with Jillian at the bar when Dan finished cleaning the kitchen. The incident with

314 ·Emma Leigh Reed

Aiden hadn't done anything to Jillian and Kelli's friendship except make it stronger. Kelli had been so unsure about Jillian's reaction after Aiden had been missing, but Jillian had assured Kelli that it was not her fault and thanked her numerous times for keeping Aiden safe. Theirs was a friendship that had weathered probably the worst of storms that there could be and still survived.

Kelli turned and smiled when she saw Dan. He approached them, suddenly acting nervous for how this conversation was going to go.

"Ready?"

"Yeah. Tell Beau we headed out." Kelli gave Jillian a hug. "Talk to you tomorrow."

Dan and Kelli walked hand-in-hand to the rocky cove where they had slowly begun to get to know each other over the past month. It was a place where glimpses of their true selves had begun to peek through. As they settled on the flat rock, Dan was nervously wiping his palms on his shorts and inhaling deeply.

"Let me start." Kelli's voice was soft.

A Time To Heal · 315

Dan nodded and gave her his full attention.

"I've never been good at relationships. They end badly all the time it seems. Even my marriage didn't work."

"That wasn't your fault, Kel."

She held up her hand. "I know deep down it was Aaron's fault for choosing to have the affairs, but I do personalize it also. It was the ultimate rejection and a slap in the face. I vowed after he walked out that I would never open my heart to another man, never allow myself to be that vulnerable again." Kelli stared out at the ocean.

It was like diamonds glancing off the top in the moonlight. She realized once again this was where she was most at harmony, not only here in North Carolina, but here in this rocky cove with Dan sitting next to her.

"I didn't want to allow myself to love again. I felt I didn't deserve it. Yet, here we are and somehow you have worked your way past my defenses without my even knowing it. Dan, somewhere along the past month, a few days, I don't know when…I fell in love with you. And for the first time, although I'm scared to death, I feel a peace about it that I have never felt before."

Kelli paused, unsure what else to say. She avoided looking at Dan and continued to be mesmerized by the waves.

"Kel, first of all, all relationships end until you find the right one. That doesn't mean you are bad at relationships, it just means you haven't had the right one yet. Secondly, I am so in love with you. I didn't plan on falling in love again. Like you, I wanted to guard my heart from ever being vulnerable again."

"So where do we go from here?" Kelli turned and faced Dan.

"We go one day at a time, together and work through all of it. All I know is I want you in my life, beside me every step of the way. Things may get rocky at times, but I want us to agree that no one runs out. We work at it and always are honest with each other."

Kelli nodded. "One day at a time."

"For the rest of our lives." Dan pulled her close. He kissed her softly, igniting a desire in her that only he could.

Emma Leigh Reed has lived in New Hampshire all her life. She has fond memories of the Maine coastline and incorporates the ocean into all her books. Her life has been touched and changed by her son's autism - she views life through a very different lens than before he was born. Growing up as an avid reader, it was only natural for Emma Leigh to turn to creating the stories for others to enjoy and has found herself an author of contemporary and romantic suspense. With a BA in Creative Writing/English, Emma Leigh enjoys sharing her knowledge with others and helping aspiring authors.

www.emmaleighreed.com

Photo Credit: Racine Photography

Made in the USA
Columbia, SC
30 August 2021